New Ghost Stories

New Ghost Stories

The Fiction Desk Anthology Series
Volume Six

Edited by Rob Redman

The Fiction Desk

First published in 2013 by The Fiction Desk Ltd.

ISBN 978-0-9927547-0-9

The Fiction Desk
PO Box 116
Rye
TN31 9DY

Please note that we do not accept postal submissions.
See our website for submissions information.

www.thefictiondesk.com

The Fiction Desk Ltd
Registered in the UK, no 07410083
Registered office: 3rd Floor, 207 Regent Street, London, W1B 3HH

Printed and bound in the UK by Imprint Digital.

Contents

Contents

Introduction

Rob Redman

Let's have some ghost stories.

Our anthologies have often drifted towards supernatural fiction, into the realms of the unexplained, like a half-asleep driver drifting briefly onto the rumble strip at the side of a quiet country road. But what happens if we don't jerk awake, don't rub our eyes and steer back to the middle of the lane? What happens if we let the car leave the road altogether?

What happens? *This happens.*

How did we get here?

This year we launched our new annual ghost story competition. The plan was originally to award first and second prizes, and to publish the two winning stories in one of our usual mixed-genre anthologies. When it came to judging the competition, though, we found we'd received so many fantastic stories, and such a diverse selection, that we couldn't properly represent them by publishing only two. A dedicated ghost story anthology was the obvious solution.

So here we have a dozen stories, including the two competition winners: Joanne Rush won first prize for 'Guests', and second prize went to Julia Patt's 'At Glenn Dale'. Among the writers that we're publishing here for the first time, you'll also see several of our regulars return: Miha Mazzini, Richard Smyth, Jason Atkinson, and Matthew Licht have all ridden in this car before, when the sun was still shining. Those were good times: we had the windows wound down and the radio turned up, we had driving sweets in paper bags from a proper sweetshop. Jason even brought his guitar.

But it's dark now, and cold. Even the moon and stars are hidden by the low cloud cover: the only thing visible outside the car is the patch of trembling road lit by the headlamps. The song they're playing on the radio is a slow one, peaceful, the musical equivalent of a thick warm duvet pulled up to your chin. I don't see the driver from where I'm sitting: is he still awake? In fact, is there anybody in the driver's seat at all?

Ah.

It might be best to hold on to something.

I was standing outside the doors of our local hospital recently when a man came out, looked down, and saw a handful of coins on the pavement. He picked them up, looked at me, and said, 'My lucky day ... apart from being in hospital, of course.' But he was lucky: lucky he wasn't at Glenn Dale ...

At Glenn Dale

Julia Patt

If you've never been to the sanatorium, just go down Route 450 a ways and turn onto Glenn Dale Road. You'll pass the police doublewide before you see the big rusting white water tower just behind the hospital proper. It might not look like much at first, a bunch of crumbling brick buildings, all boarded up and caving in, the whole place discarded a long time ago. But it's a large property: more than two hundred acres, about two dozen buildings originally, though most of the wooden ones — the doctors' gabled houses, the chapel, maintenance sheds — have rotted through and collapsed over the years. From overhead, it would look like a town, long abandoned; a main square with small intersecting avenues, slowly decaying and disappearing. But the big attractions remain in the middle of it all: the hospital and the children's ward, both three stories tall. Big brick industrial monsters with shattered windows.

We know just about all there is to know about Glenn Dale. We have made it our business to know, from the hospital's official history (built in '34, condemned and closed in '82) to the speculated (its stint as a mental institution) to what most would call fiction: the stories everyone tells about Glenn Dale, the stories about the ghosts. Some nights, when it's warm enough, we walk out to the sanatorium alone on its hill, settle ourselves in one of the corridors or the abandoned dormitories, build a small fire, pass the flask around, and retell the stories.

There's the one about the Shrieker, a woman whose husband died here in the forties, who was so overcome with grief that she died too, and on the anniversary of their deaths, she goes howling through the halls, wailing and tearing at her hair. Or the Orderly, a guy from the seventies in blue-green scrubs, porno 'stache and all, who walks the halls, rattling the doors, telling the patients to keep quiet, it's lights out, and all the while his scrubs are stained dark, and his head lolls against his shoulder. There are the swarms of patients from the TB days, the ones who came from the cities to die in the country, most of them silent and shaking with coughing, their mouths frothing red, their eyes glassy dark. They mostly move in groups, the lot of them staggering down the hall, mindless, whoever they were erased by pain and illness and death. (We've heard that if one of them touches you, you'll get it too.)

But our best stories are the recent ones, the accidents after the hospital closed. The first one was in '83, just ten months after the state condemned Glenn Dale on account of the asbestos, when a girl came here with her friends. They say that she tripped and fell out the window on the third floor in the children's ward, but we know better. We know there were giggles and whispers behind the door, the touch of small, cold hands on hers. Maybe it was the small, cold hands that did it; maybe she jumped. No one knows for certain. More than a decade later, there was the boy, one of the nonbelievers, who tumbled through the water-rotted floor, broke his leg on the way down. He waited in the dark for hours until someone found him, chilled and gibbering about voices in the dark. There are the trophy-hunters too, dumb enough to take souvenirs — abandoned teddy bears and shoes and even prosthetic limbs from the hospital basement — who ended up watched by white-eyed ghouls in the night.

But our favourite, the story we tell over and over, the one we all know by heart, whispered across the fire on the darkest, loneliest nights, Glenn Dale close around us, its years of occupants listening, pausing when we pause, shivering when we shiver — our favourite story is the one about the Fitz and Mark Dooley.

The Fitz graduated a few years before we did, but we all remember him. He was one of those people everyone knows, at least in high school: a tall gangly guy, not so much good looking as distinct, the sort of face you could pick out in a police line-up. All the girls flirted with him and he'd kissed most of them open mouthed in front of the lockers at one time or another, but none of them ever took him home or held his hand. See, everyone knew the Fitz, liked him too, but we never felt close to him. He wasn't even the kind of guy you could call by his first name: everyone just called him the Fitz or Fitzer, like the football coaches did.

In the Fitz's junior year, a new kid came to school, Mark Dooley, who moved to Bowie from Seattle. The girls mooned over him because he was from the West Coast and had this dark curly hair and these sensitive puppy eyes, brown as bullshit. It seemed pretty clear from the start that Mark Dooley and the Fitz weren't going to be friends, but no one expected the fight, not with a goodie like Mark and not even with Fitzer, who was never uptight about anything except for his older brother Eric, and anything to do with Glenn Dale.

In their day, back when we were all little kids, the Fitzer brothers had a longstanding claim on Glenn Dale. In fact, some say the Fitz was on his way to the sanatorium since he could walk. By the time he hit kindergarten, he and Eric were sneaking off to explore buildings. When Eric was at Bowie High School and Fitzer was just a gawky seventh grader, they were already the grand-time champions of most nights spent on the grounds. Even people who didn't love Fitzer — and there were plenty, although not in our crowd — respected his claim on Glenn Dale. To this day, if he showed up and told us to get lost, we would. It's a safe bet that will never happen, but still, on principle, we would.

You could say, maybe, that Mark Dooley just didn't know any better.

The fight happened in eighth period World History with Mrs Showler, who was forty and getting fat and always had runs in her stockings. She was okay as teachers go, never gave pop quizzes because she didn't want us to hate her and didn't mind if a paper was late. She seemed happy enough to get through her lessons without incident. Problem was, Mark Dooley had been giving the Fitz this kind of *look* — angry and a little challenging — all week, since the talk about Glenn Dale and Halloween started up around school. Laidback as he was, the Fitz wasn't the kind of person to let this stand, so during eighth period, he swapped seats one by one until he came to the middle row and tapped Mark on the shoulder. 'Hey Dooley,' he hissed. 'The fuck's your problem?'

'There's no problem,' Mark said, without looking back.

'You know exactly what I'm talking about, dude.'

Moments passed before Mark turned to look at the Fitz. He pursed his lips, his brows drawn, curls hanging over his eyes. Finally he asked, 'What's the big deal with Glenn Dale?' He said it as if Fitzer was personally responsible for the place's existence. 'It's just some shitty, run-down heap.'

About then the kids around them started paying attention. No one had called the Fitz out about Glenn Dale since fourth grade, and that kid went home with the worst bloody nose anyone had ever seen. But the Fitz didn't hit Mark — yet. He exhaled loudly through his nose and unclenched his hands. His voice went kind of cool and soft. 'And what would you know about it?' he asked.

Mark Dooley smiled a small, smug smile and shrugged. 'I'm just saying, compared to Charles Manson's house or a '49 gold rush ghost town, it's not really that impressive.'

'Right,' the Fitz said. 'If it's so lame here, why don't you just get your parents to move back to San Francisco?' A few people laughed, and, satisfied, the Fitz started to move back to his seat.

'Seattle,' Mark Dooley said.

'What?' Fitzer turned around so that he was looming over Mark.

Mrs Showler had stopped her lesson by then, as the discussion was getting on the loud side. She held her piece of chalk as if it might save her. 'Look, boys,' she started to say. 'Enough chatter. Let's get back to — '

'I'm from Seattle,' Mark repeated.

Fitzer snorted. He put his palms on the desk behind Mark, leaned over, and stuck his face in the new guy's. 'And I don't give a shit,' he said. 'Faggot.'

That's when Mark Dooley punched the Fitz in the face.

The guys only got a few hits in before security broke it up, but Fitzer walked around with a black eye for two weeks after that, and Mark Dooley had a split lip that all the girls cooed over. It was only later, in detention, that the matter got solved. A note that Mark's parents found after the fact: *Glenn Dale. Friday. Sundown.*

There's some debate about whether what happened after was the Fitz's fault. After all, he invited Mark Dooley out to Glenn Dale. But, as others point out, Mark threw the first punch. In the end, we say, they both went so it doesn't matter, not really.

On the night in question, the Fitz arrived on foot. Even though it was a warm October, he wore his black sweatshirt, hood drawn, his backpack secure over both shoulders. For Fitzer, Glenn Dale provisions included a six-pack of National Bohemian beer, a box of Ritz peanut butter crackers, a lighter, a flashlight with extra batteries, his brother's old pocketknife, a disposable camera, and an extra pair of sneakers (the Fitz hated wet shoes). He and Eric had always packed carefully so that nothing would give them away, and the Fitz had strictly held to these traditions.

Fitzer hid in the bamboo stand behind the hospital until Mark Dooley showed. The other guy kept close to the tree line as he approached, guiding his bike, baseball cap pulled low over his eyes, one of those big metal flashlights in his back pocket, a duffel slung over one shoulder. Fitzer watched as Mark parked his bike in the trees and piled some branches around it. When he had finished, Fitzer stepped out from the bamboo and said quietly, 'You're late, dude.'

Mark jumped and looked around. The sun had pretty much set by then, the sky all smoky purple like it is during an Indian summer. They were in the main courtyard; the largest hospital building loomed just in front of them, the children's ward farther up and to the right, the chapel and the nurses' quarters down the hill. The water tower threw its spidery shadow. Mark took in the 'No Trespassing' signs, the boarded up entrances, the jagged, shattered windows. 'Wasn't going to stand you up,' he said. 'Don't worry.'

Fitzer rolled his eyes and laughed, but kept his voice low. Most people get caught at Glenn Dale because they get wrapped up in the uneasy freedom of the place, but the Fitz never forgot where he was. 'C'mon, Dooley,' he said.

They entered the hospital through a back door, where the Fitz had long ago pulled away the boards and propped it open just enough with a cement block. The front entrances were all sealed. They stood together in a stairwell: cement walls layered with spray-painted graffiti, broken glass crunching beneath their sneakers, the warped metal stairs winding upwards next to them. Someone had blocked the entrance to the first floor with a massive, rusting, metal bookcase; they had tried a similar approach with the staircase itself, using a pile of old chairs, but Fitzer pulled one loose and slipped through. He moved gingerly. The stairs groaned; the whole line of them trembled. Some of the bolts had rusted through after that year's hurricane season and the frame was beginning to pull away from the wall.

He led Mark Dooley up to the second floor, motioning for him to move slowly and watch his step. Their shoes made empty noises on the metal. Reaching the second floor, they stepped into the hallway. Fitzer never camped in the rooms like some people: there was always the possibility you'd get trapped behind a blocked exit, and you'd be stuck until the patrolmen heard you and sent you home. The hospital buildings are old, and even though the exteriors are brick, there's a lot on the inside that is flammable, and campfires can get out of hand; we know that from experience. The Fitz walked down the hallway a ways, letting Mark glance in the old treatment rooms and wards, the overturned lockers and beds here and there, a coat rack hanging off the wall by some loose screws, a gurney and a toilet seat discarded in one corner. Finding a spot in the hall he liked, the Fitz started to settle in, piled up newspapers in a battered old wastebasket, blackened with smoke, and cracked open a can of Natty Boh.

The Fitz flicked his lighter — a small, cheap plastic deal, he didn't smoke — and the newspapers caught pretty well, greasy smoke rising to the ceiling, creeping out the broken windows in the hall. In the wavering light, Mark got a better look around, the sickly green linoleum floor, stained and scarred, puckering at the corners. The walls, once whitewashed and now streaked with grime, were covered almost entirely by graffiti: Sara and Pete Forever / Charlie was here / Fuck you dude / Lisa is a skank, etc. Fitzer took a long draw on his beer and cocked his head at Mark, who was still standing.

He cleared his throat and asked, 'Aren't we going to ... you know ... look for ghosts and stuff?'

Fitzer laughed out loud, snorting a little on his beer as he did so. He shook his head a few times, as if to clear the humour from it, and even wiped his eyes. 'I'm sorry, Agent Mulder. Would you like a tour?'

Mark frowned. He hitched the duffel up a little farther over his shoulder. 'Well. I guess.' He stopped, still frowning down at the Fitz like he was a particularly difficult trigonometry problem and this was the weighted midterm exam. 'Isn't that why we're here? To prove whether this place is haunted or not?'

'Dude. We're here because you're a snotty West Coast asshole who picks fights with the wrong people because he's pissed he had to move.' Fitzer took another swig and belched, looking pleased. He raised a hand when Mark started to protest. 'It's true. But don't you worry any, hon. We don't have to go to the ghosts. The ghosts will come to us. Glenn Dale is haunted. If you want to go play Ghostbusters, knock yourself out, but I'm staying right here to wait for them. Trust me, I know what works.'

Mark stood there a minute, a few feet away from Fitzer. He swallowed visibly a few times, looking from the sprawling guy in front him to the dark stairway behind them. Then at the series of doorways along the halls, thinking about what he'd heard, from kids like us, about collapsed ceilings and broken glass and people who got lost and were never heard from again.

He moved a few steps closer and sat down, crossing his legs under him like we're all taught to do in kindergarten. The Fitz offered him a beer. Mark stared at him for a moment, suspecting a trick, but finally he took the can. It was cold. He popped it open and tipped it back. He looked again at the shadows flickering on the walls. Eventually he said, 'So this place is pretty cool, haunted or not.'

The Fitz finished his beer and crunched the can in one hand. He looked around. Everybody knows the look he had when he was at Glenn Dale: precisely like a king surveying his lands. There was pride and possessiveness and something softer, like nostalgia, maybe even like love. He accepted this peace offering from Mark Dooley. 'Yeah, man,' he said, smiling a little. 'Sure is.'

Mark watched the Fitz as he opened another can. 'How many times have you been here, do you think?' Through the windows that weren't boarded, he could see the sky getting darker, stars showing through the tree branches. He thought he heard a car on Glenn Dale Road, though from inside the buildings it was impossible to be sure. Glenn Dale eats you up, if you aren't careful: it's easy to lose track of time, to forget the world outside, even if the wind is blowing through the broken windows. You just become part of it, somehow, part of the ruin of it. All the sad stories are your stories, and the scary ones too.

Fitzer laughed again, though it was nicer sounding now, a genuine laugh. 'I have no idea. I've been coming here as long as I can remember, a few times a year at least. Dozens of times. Maybe even a hundred or two, I don't know. You know, one time we went a whole weekend here.'

'You and your brother?' Mark asked. He rummaged in his duffel and pulled out a package of beef jerky. He offered some to Fitzer.

More laughter from the Fitz. 'Really roughing it, aren't you, Dooley?' He took some and spoke as he chewed. 'Yeah, me and Eric. It was the summer of ... '98? His sophomore year of high school. We told our mom that we were staying at a friend's house for the weekend.' He paused here to take another drink. 'Instead we just went down the road, spent the whole weekend walking the tunnels and searching the rooms. We spent hours in the boiler room; they still had the original riveted machine from the thirties, coal-fed and everything. Eric showed me how they put those things together — they were *monsters*, dude. It was the coolest thing.' Fitzer stopped abruptly. He had never really told that story to anyone before, not because it wasn't interesting, but because there were no ghosts in it, and no police chases.

Mark edged a little closer to the fire, extending his fingers towards the sputtering flames even though it wasn't cold at all. Everyone feels that way in Glenn Dale at some point or another, the need to seek light and warmth, to shield yourself from the deeper shadows in the corners of the rooms. 'And you didn't get caught?' he asked.

Fitzer shrugged. He drank some more and pulled back to look at the can, the gold label and white script, as if it was an artefact from another age. 'Dude, they're PG county cops, not the LAPD.'

As if to emphasise his point, a door slammed shut on the floor above them. Both boys jumped and then immediately checked to see if the other guy had jumped too. They sat in silence for a moment, listening to their rabbiting heartbeats, both a little ashamed to have been caught off guard. Mark stared at the Fitz, maybe trying to discern if this was some sort of prank, a test, revenge for what he had done in Showler's class. Fitzer had gotten himself under control; after the initial shock, he looked nonchalant.

Mark tried to laugh it off — one of those breathless, panicky laughs — and shook his head, maybe denying that he had heard anything at all. 'How many times do I have to tell you that I'm not from California?' His voice cracked.

In the dark, the Fitz's smile looked ghoulish. He licked his lips and said, 'You're all the same.'

Mark Dooley snorted his beer. 'Hey, fuck you!' But he was laughing, too, the kind of laugh that follows fear, relieved and embarrassed.

On the floor below them, hinges rattled and something small fell to the ground and shattered, one of those old-fashioned glass syringes. Fitzer recognized the sound. Mark flinched, but the Fitz was cool this time. He waved a hand to show Mark it was okay.

That sound, that tinkling, that shattering, was the ghost everyone called the Betty. She looked just like the flappers in old movies, her hair in a close bob, her lips painted, but in a housecoat, blood on the sleeves from all her coughing. The Betty was pretty clumsy, stumbling into stuff a lot and knocking it over. She wouldn't talk to you either, but sometimes would go to the window and light a long, thin cigarette, the kind in a Cruella De Vil holder.

'Where is your brother, anyway?' Mark asked after a while. 'Is he in college or something?' Mark wanted to hear something other than the ghosts, wanted to hear a solid, human voice, even if it was Fitzer's.

At this point the Fitz went all quiet, looking into the dying, greasy fire like the answer to Mark's question was in there instead of his head. Then he started talking as if Mark Dooley had asked a different question. 'You know, no one likes to come here in the winter. It's cold and the stairs can get icy and snow blows in the windows sometimes. But Eric and me ... we would still come here. One winter ... we were both pretty young, all bundled up and stuff –' At this point, he pulled a flask from an inner pocket and took a swig; he was aware of Mark's attention on him. 'We didn't think the patrol would be out so much, but Daisy, a big old shepherd they had then, she got a whiff of us and started barking her head off.'

More crashing, upstairs this time, just above their heads. This was the guy everyone called the General, a little old guy with big handlebar moustaches, right out of a John Wayne Western. Mark jumped again. Without meaning to, he grabbed for the Fitz's sleeve, something, anything that was real, that wasn't Glenn Dale.

Fitzer continued as if he hadn't noticed. 'So we started running, we ducked into the children's ward because there are some closets up there you can hide in pretty well when you're a kid. But we got into the ground floor and there was this bum lying there.' He took another drink from the flask, pausing to pass it to Mark. 'He wasn't moving at all. He had this layer of frost on him. Made him look like he was made of glass.' He paused. 'Honest to God, dude, I saw his spirit pull itself right out of his body. First real ghost I ever saw.'

Mark shuddered a little as the whisky burned down his throat. 'Shit.' He coughed. 'What's the deal, man? Where is your brother, anyway? He's not dead too, is he?' It was meant to come out like a joke, but the Fitz didn't acknowledge the question, and Mark got this sick kind of expression, the kind of face you make when you've put your foot in something serious. Sitting in Glenn Dale, listening to the ghosts, looking at Fitzer's quiet expression, Mark wanted more than anything to be home, not his house in Bowie, but *home* in Seattle – the clean cut of the buildings, the white mountains around it all — with his friends, who didn't believe in ghosts or have dead brothers. He hadn't meant to pick a fight with the Fitz; he honestly hadn't, had only been bored with all the Glenn Dale talk, thought it was all small town bullshit, but he hadn't understood then.

The Fitz kept going. 'That was the closest we ever got to being caught. We were scared, but we went and hid anyway and when Daisy and the patrolman showed up, they got so busy with the ... you know, the guy, that they forgot all about us. Eric didn't want to go back for a while after that.' He rubbed his hands together. Then he looked at Mark and shrugged.

'Fitzer. Eric's *not* dead. Is he?' Mark needed to know, without understanding why, that Eric Fitzer was okay. Maybe if Eric Fitzer was okay, Mark Dooley could be okay.

The Fitz laughed at his bug-eyed look. 'Dude. My brother isn't dead. He's overseas.' He took another drink after this particularly sticky word: overseas.

'Overseas?'

'You know.' The Fitz gestured vaguely eastward, where the sun would rise at the end of the whole thing. 'Over there. Where they're fighting. Iraq. Afghanistan.'

'Oh,' said Mark. He looked at his hands. 'Man. I'm sorry. I'm so sorry, I —'

Fitzer held up a hand and said, 'Don't sweat it, dude.' The thing with the Fitz was he never wanted you to feel bad for him. He wanted you to forget it. 'It's not a big deal.'

They sat there in awkward silence for a long time, Mark Dooley thinking he was the world's biggest douche, the Fitz thinking about Eric over in the East, wherever he was.

Then, down the hall, less than fifty feet from them, a door slammed. And another. And a third. And just as quickly, they creaked opened again, one by one. Then it happened again. And again. Mark jumped. The Fitz reached out to steady him, a friendly gesture; they were sitting pretty close, hearts pounding together.

After the doors stopped, Fitzer felt Mark Dooley's hands under the hood of his sweatshirt, his fingers clasping behind his neck very gently. His first thought was that the hands were pretty cold for a warm October night: Mark's skin was clammy, as if he had broken into a sweat. Then, who knows, maybe Fitzer was thinking that Dooley had decided to strangle him after all. We can guarantee that he didn't expect what really happened: Mark Dooley planted one on the Fitz, one of those lengthy open-mouthed kisses the Fitz had shared with so many girls over the years.

Maybe it was the booze, maybe it was the night and the ghosts, and maybe it was none of the above. But there was the kiss, a long kiss, Fitzer in his usual slouch, Mark Dooley pulling him close, kneeling next to him, and they were both a little breathless when it was over.

The Fitz stared, his jaw working as he tried to speak, but what could he say? In the pathetic firelight, you would have thought that he was *blushing*, our Fitzer, a delicate pink spreading along his cheekbones. Finally, he spoke, his voice hoarse. 'What did you — ?'

Mark looked at him helplessly. Then he kissed him again, a little harder this time, the two of them tasting whisky and Natty Boh and Ritz peanut butter crackers and beef jerky. All new. And then Mark asked, 'What's your name, Fitzer?'

And the Fitz, looking stunned, maybe feeling a little bit like those girls he'd kissed in the hall. 'It's Danny,' he said. 'Danny Lewis Fitzer.'

Everyone around here knows that, of course, and it's what's on Fitzer's diploma from the county, but it was strange to say it, stranger to hear it said aloud, like a confession.

'Danny, I — '

The Fitz laughed, surprised at the sound of it. He touched his mouth a little, as if to make sure it was still the same. 'Uh, dude. Look.' He laughed again, a giddy noise. 'Nobody calls me Danny unless he wants his nose broken.' He leaned over to Mark again, maybe for another kiss, but pulled back quick when Mark leaned in too, expectant. 'What the hell, man?' the Fitz demanded.

'Da — Fitzer,' Mark corrected himself. 'I swear I didn't plan this. It was just —' He laughed too, a kind of desperate sound. 'I didn't even like you. I thought all this was bullshit. I thought you were just some asshole.' He got up, moving away from Fitzer. He started walking away, down the hall.

'Hey, Dooley. *Mark*. Wait up,' Fitzer said, getting to his feet, but he'd had a little more to drink than Mark and was slower getting going, his legs full of wet sand, it seemed. It's fine, he thought. I'll catch up.

But then they were there, the legion of them, Glenn Dale's dead, between Mark Dooley and the far end of the hall, their vacant eyes staring, their lips flecked with blood, their faces grey, empty, and they were reaching out for Mark, cold hands extended, maybe a hundred, maybe a thousand of them. And Mark Dooley, who didn't believe in ghosts, turned and ran, ran past Fitzer, who couldn't quite catch him, stumbling, who could only yell, helpless, for him to be careful, to watch out for the stairs.

Those stairs, they were just sitting against the wall, really, held on by nothing. It didn't matter much if you were a normal-sized person and you took your time. Mark Dooley wasn't a big guy, but he hit the stairs heavy, at a run, and the whole thing came down with him in half a second. The Fitz was following so close that he almost went down too and had to catch himself on the doorframe, still calling Mark's name.

He never told anybody that the reason he stopped going to Glenn Dale is that every time he set foot in one of the old buildings after that, he saw a totally new ghost: Mark Dooley falling into the darkness from the rusty stairs, arms pedalling the air as if he'd learned to fly, his mouth still warm from what they'd shared only a moment or two before.

Or maybe he just outgrew the place. Most of us do.

*In Eloise Shepherd's story, Jack is losing control over his family.
Is it the cracks in his life that let something else in? To put it
another way, do ghosts create fear, or does fear create ghosts?*

Journeyman

Eloise Shepherd

'Dad!' Joe's yelling out in the hall. It's day already, but still cold.
Used to be easy waking up but these days my head hurts.

'Da-ad,' he yells again and I'm up. Stumbling out and he's
stood there rattling the bathroom door, legs crossed over, bursting
for a piss. He has his duvet wrapped around him.

'Dad, Mark's in the bathroom and he's been in there forever
and he won't let me in.'

I sigh.

'Mark. Get out of there,' I say. He doesn't say a word and Joe's
fidgeting behind me. I'm worried if I don't do something he's
gonna piss himself in the hall.

'Mark, come on, what are you doing in there? I'm counting to
ten.'

Not a sound. I'd expect him to yell something back but he
doesn't say a thing. What if he had a fit or something, collapsed.

The lock is screwed hard into the wall — I know because I drilled it in myself — but I can bust it with my shoulder.

'Right, that's ten.'

The door gives easily. The room is white and bright. Mark's in there alright. Joe rushes in behind me and pisses loudly. And Mark's asleep in the dry bath in boxers and a grey T-shirt, half under a blanket. He's pale.

My heart gets tight.

'Mark? Mark, stop fucking messing, okay?'

He doesn't move. I bend down beside him in the bath and grab his arm. He's warm, thank god. I shake him.

'Mark.'

His eyelids twitch. The boy's drunk? Thirteen years old and drunk already? He splutters and wakes up, eyes screwed with the light.

'Dad.' He tries to sit himself up, skinny little arms tensing.

'What in hell are you doing?'

He says nowt. Just looks at me with big scared eyes.

Joe's off back downstairs for breakfast, says nothing. Mark struggles to get out with his stiff limbs that have been wedged there maybe all night. I lean in to help, but he shakes his head and struggles on. It feels awkward. He heads through to his room. I just follow.

'Mark, have you been drinking son?'

He looks at me with cloudy eyes.

'No, Dad, I swear.'

'What are you sick, then?'

He shakes his head and I don't know what it is that he isn't saying. 'What then?'

He shakes his head again and squeezes his eyes shut.

'Mark, what is it?'

'I couldn't, I couldn't sleep in here.'

'Why?'

He just looks at me and rubs his eyes.

I let him get back to sleep for a while in his own bed.

By the time I get downstairs Joe is through his second bowl of cereal. I pull on my sweater, which is drying on the radiator.

'Are you training later, Dad?'

'Course, I'll head up there around two, wanna come?'

'Can I go to Mum's?'

I nod. These days they both can't seem to get enough of going to their mum's. Time was Mark would sit on his Xbox long as I'd let him but now he's keen to get gone.

I wait for Mark to wake up. I shave. My nose in the bathroom mirror is crooked and you can see the shape of the straight right I walked into that broke it. I know better than that now.

I don't know why it gets so cold in this house. I pay enough in bloody gas bills but all the heat seems to leak and leave us shivering. I got into the guts of the boiler but I couldn't figure a thing wrong. The engineer came and said he had it sorted, but that was bollocks. He's coming back tomorrow. The water on my face is so cold washing away the stubble. My eyes throb. Who knows if it's from the cold or from sparring the other night.

Out in the hall there's no noise from Mark's room; he's still asleep. The radiator clunks, so it must be doing something. I head back downstairs and Joe's still at the kitchen table with his back to me.

'... can't talk to Dad ...' he's saying as I walk in, then he freezes and looks round at me. There's no one else there.

'What can't you tell me?' I say and he looks awkward and tense, his small muscles draw together in his shoulders.

'Nowt.'

The phone's on the hook on the other side of the room and he doesn't have a mobile.

'What's with you?'

Joe shrugs his shoulder and doesn't look at me. He takes his empty cereal bowl to the sink and washes it.

Mark comes down a couple of hours later in one of my club hoodies.

'I'm dropping you both off at your mum's on my way to training,' I tell him. He just nods. Pours himself a glass of cold water. The kid's taller than me almost but he's still skinny like a child. His hair blond like Marie's.

They both get in the car and I drive them over. They're saying nothing. I don't go in to see Marie because the past year or more we only have the same conversation. Awkward not angry these days, yeah, but it just goes round and round and I can't bear it. And he's always there — in the kitchen or something, being so nice to the kids — with his unbroken nose and his Downton fucking Abbey accent. Mark, he hasn't got time for that, but my little Joe, after visits he gushes. I watch the pair of them walk into the house and drive off.

The gym's so warm. I don't much have a trainer anymore because it isn't like anyone is expecting anything. I get booked to lose, these days, and you can't turn up your nose at that, it's good money. So I train myself and my promoter's happy to have me there, to pad records, to take the fall. In 1999 I was Amateur Boxing Association of England Champion, light middleweight, but that's a fair long time ago now. Just need to look after myself, no use taking too many shots.

Boxing clears my head. I get warm, proper warm head to toe. And the heavy bag shakes because I can do it, I can box — I can dazzle you. Just mostly here, not in the ring. In the ring I look after myself.

The Russians bring me in sparring with one of their guys. He's a big guy but still, and then sudden quick and at you. None of the side to side shimmy. Inside the head guard his eyes are big and black and he stares at me. I focus on his forehead and I keep moving. Slipping my shots in. Much taller so I'm in and under, at his ribs and his body but he gets wise to that, throws uppercuts. Good ones too, and they're hard to pull off. When he lands a flush one, the impact vibrates up through my jaw, my skull and as always the pain is like being squeezed and punctured but I'm used to that, I can shake it off. The last one he lands feels like a bell ringing in my skull and his black vest suddenly twinkles with little yellow dots. I stay upright.

After sparring he says nothing, unloops his wraps and nods to his coach. I shower at the gym, it's warmer.

I wait for ten minutes outside Marie's house in the car. I can't bring myself to knock when they've been playing happy families. And Marie, she gives me this look and I can't tell her, I can't say I'm sorry, after all, I'm sorry. I just keep my mouth shut and I look at the ground.

The kids eat fish fingers, peas, and chips for their teas, watching TV. They had a good lunch at their mum's but I want to give them a treat. The chips are so hot you have to blow on them before you can touch them. I hope they'll help keep them warm. I go into the kitchen and put the laundry on, get washed up. Before Marie left she did all of this. I was a lazy shit but it wasn't because I didn't love her, she's wrong about that.

My fingers crinkle up from the water. I refilled the washing up bottle with water and there's barely enough soap to shift a thing. I leave everything to dry and press my hands against the tea towel. It needs a wash. Everything always needs a wash.

I walk back through into the front room and my eyes must have been blinded by the bright in the kitchen and then the dim in here because for a second I could be sure there was someone else sitting with the boys in there. Someone in Marie's old chair. It leaves me with a wrong feeling in my gut.

I put Joe to bed and he brushes his teeth without being asked. I pat his head and he smiles at me. Downstairs, Mark knows we are going to have words. He's sitting hunched over, watching music television turned down low. It's just a buzz in the background.

'What happened last night, Mark?' He shrugs and doesn't look at me.

'Were you drinking?'

'You are fucking obsessed with me drinking Dad, will you give over. I'm not the one who's bloody drinking. I was just tired.'

'Tired? So you slept in the bath? You're not making any sense. Do you think I didn't try and get things past my dad when I was your age?'

He just shrugs.

'Why did you say you didn't want to sleep in your room?'

His jaw tightens.

'Dunno.'

I feel like I'm in the one in the corner keeping my hands up to protect my head.

'Why won't you talk to me?' I say.

'It was just a bit warmer in there alright? That's all. I was really cold.'

I don't believe him. Something else is going on here.

I go and put the laundry to spin again because in this house it takes long enough to bloody dry. Mark boots up his Xbox and I let him sit up a bit, it's Sunday tomorrow. I've checked my bottles and nothing is missing, nothing has been watered down.

I have a glass myself, I need it, just some whisky in a mug with a drop of water. Stop at two though, always keep telling myself I don't need much. Just a nightcap, nothing to get worried about, not like sometimes. I've had a hard day.

Going to bed I still don't feel like Mark's safe and I can't place why. For a while I can't keep still. It's so cold outside the duvet and inside it's too warm and I can't figure that. I hear Mark coming up the stairs to bed and knocking off the light in the hall. His bedroom door closes.

The radiator grumbles at me. Then knocks like there's someone trying to get out. Sometimes the knocking comes so close together it sounds like laughter.

I throw my hand out over the pillow and the cold comes so quickly, all the little hairs rising. I sit up straight in bed and somehow know to turn to the door just as it opens. It opens so slowly but there's nothing there. Outside on the landing there's little footsteps. When he was little, Joe used to come in, sleep in our bed, maybe the same now. I get up and pad over to the door but he isn't looking for me. Slips into Mark's room and I hear his low voice.

'Mark,' he whispers. My heart beats fast. Stood just inside the door I can see the back of his head but he isn't turning round. 'Mark, I'm scared, can I come in with you?'

Then he disappears and the door closes. It's quiet again. I get back into bed because outside I'll be shivering. Why are they both so scared? What's happening in this house, the pair of them are too scared to sleep in their own beds? Something isn't right but I don't know what.

At eight the heating engineer arrives. We just can't keep on going and be this cold. It gets in your bones.

'Can't figure what's wrong, mate,' he says. 'Everything is going where it should. After all that work the other week I just don't understand.'

He seems embarrassed, coming all this way with nowt to show for it. We both stand in the kitchen looking at the boiler. Pilot light's on, you can even hear the water heating up but nothing, no heat. I reset the thing again.

'I don't think it'll help,' the engineer says, closing down his little British Gas laptop.

'Yeah, but it can't hurt, right?'

'I guess not. We're going to need to get a team out here or something. Could be your whole system needs replacing.'

I nod.

'Mate, this is going to sound stupid but do you believe in ghosts?'

The engineer looks at me coldly.

'What?'

'It's this cold right, and the radiators at night. Something isn't right.'

'Yeah, there's a problem with your boiler.'

'Yeah forget I said anything.'

He's still looking at me funny and I don't trust him. Stupid to say a word. By ten he's off and it's just me and the boys. Joe is pretending he didn't sleep in Mark's bed last night, and I let him. It's easier that way.

'So who are you fighting next week, Dad?' Joe asks and I get a sinking feeling because I don't like explaining to him what I do.

'Oh I can't remember. Some kid not long out of the amateurs.'

He doesn't ask if I'm gonna win, because all of us know the answer to that.

'Dad are you alright?'

'What? Yeah? Course — why?'

He shakes his head and looks down.

I make a pretext of going upstairs for something. Crossing the landing I see her. White T-shirt and grey dense flesh, a slick black bob. Just standing and standing in the boys' room. Instead of eyes she's got bone white sockets but I know she's looking at me. Her skin's like white paper — bloodless. I rub my eyes and look back. She's gone.

I'm panicking. Can't deny I'm panicking. I'm in deep water and it's just me here, me and the boys.

I need another drink just a little something just to steady my nerves. A little taste that's all because I can't think straight and my hands are trembling and what if she — this thing — what if it comes back?

I call Marie. Stupid, yeah I know, but she's the only one I'm used to turning to. It takes her five rings to answer and I'm just staring at the bedroom door.

'Hello.'

'Marie.'

'What's the matter?' I can tell she's caught that note in my voice.

'Marie, there's something in the house.'

'What?'

'I don't fucking know.'

She keeps quiet a minute and I know there's something she's working out if she can say.

'I think you need to see a doctor.'

I don't understand.

'Jack, when you're hit in the face again and again for fifteen years — more — do you expect your brain to stand up to that? Do you think we haven't noticed, how you've changed recently? You're scaring the boys, you're drinking more and more. They aren't stupid.'

'There's nothing wrong with my brain. It isn't me the boys are scared of, it's this thing. It's here Marie — I've seen it.'

'I know that's what you think, Jack, but you need help. I'll come with you. Just go talk to someone. It can't hurt can it? ... Listen, Tony's got a friend at the hospital, a consultant —'

I hang up the phone. I can tell she's had her little speech and been rehearsing it, just looking for the right moment. She calls back and the ringtone is very high and gets right inside my head. I can't bear it. I turn it off but she calls back again so I just slam the thing against the wall. I can't help it. The sound dies. I smash it so hard it comes to pieces in my hand. Glass screen smashed to shit and all the thin pieces on the carpet. Fuck, it's not even insured.

My head aches. I can hear the sound of Mark's Xbox downstairs. I walk to the window. She's there. That thing. She's stood in the garden, stock still.

I feel like I'm underwater, like when the ref's counting to ten and you want to stand up but your legs ain't got it.

I run downstairs. The boys look round and yeah they're scared I can see the fear in them. I run out into the garden. Whatever this thing is I can stand up to it. But it's gone. I stand there for a second, and then I turn back to the house. The door closes softly and slowly. I walk towards it though I know, I know.

It's locked dead like rock it won't move. I can't get back in.

*The nature of ghosts is as variable as their appearance.
For example, does the narrator of Oli Hadfield's 'Tom'
technically count as a ghost? You'd have to ask him ...*

Tom

Oli Hadfield

It's no wonder Tom can't sleep. He doesn't shut up. He just lays there asking about this, that, and the other. 'What should I do about them?' he says. 'Why don't they leave me alone? Can't you talk to them?' Well, no I can't, sunshine, because I'm just a part of your little nugget. This kid here's got more potential than others. I know what he's thinking when he sleeps. He dreams about films. He wants to be a writer/director. He wants to replace ET as a sci-fi classic. He's got stories flying around his noodle, and they're shit, but they're sparks. That's what I tell him tonight, that he's not supposed to be a genius from the beginning.

'So when'll I make it?' he asks.

'When you grow up,' I say. 'You'll work on it and work on it and eventually, you'll create something that shines.'

'Like a star.'

'Go to sleep, kid.' I put my arm across him until he falls asleep. I never last much longer than him when he goes.

I don't usually see him in the mornings. For that hour or so before he walks to school, I'm gone while he tries to pluck up some courage in the mirror. I imagine it hurts to watch a twelve-year-old do something like that.

But today I'm up early. His mother has toast on the dining table for him. He eats it up while his mother reads texts off her phone that are coming from his dad. She reads aloud that he wants to meet her. Not a date, but a coffee and chat, enough to make her moan and dance on the spot.

Next thing I know we're on the playground. It's almost nine and he's walking towards registration.

'What's up?' I ask.

He looks at me with a familiar expression. 'Over there,' he says, and points towards the opposite end of the field, where Jack Finnegan is sat on a bench with three other blank name-tags.

'Just keep walking.' I pat him on the back, and keep my eyes on the others. They see him. Tom just looks straight ahead as if he hasn't noticed them.

'Oi, Tom!' says Jack. 'Tom!' Tom ignores him, and walks deliberately to the main building. 'Hey Tom, come here. Wanna show you something.' They've done this before, shown him a picture of a decapitated man. Tom's queasy and it gives them a few kicks to see his face squirm in disgust, so they come up with ways to trick him into seeing it.

He gets into registration. A few kids say hey to him and he says hey back, but he sits alone and calls 'here' when his name's read out, all the while drawing a robot on a piece of paper. A kid next to him steals it.

'Why've you drawn this?' he says, laughing and waving it about so the rest of the kids can see it. Tom snatches it back, embarrassed.

I'm with him through English, discussing a book he's just read. Tom's been struggling to read lately because his mind is on Jack, and also Danny Braithwaite who pushes him about, and Carl Holloway who pulls his pants down in the changing rooms before and after Games. But he listens, and takes a mental note of what Mrs Atkinson says about Shakespeare's Globe Theatre.

'Tom,' says Mrs Atkinson. 'Are you listening?'

'Yes, Miss,' he says. She approaches him, and looks at his notes. He's also been updating his robot. She crumples it up and throws it in the bin. With her back turned, there's a chorus of 'ooo!' and the kid swings a ruler through me and onto his back. He ignores all of this, and for the rest of the lesson sits in silence.

It's also hard for us to play together during breaks, so it's good that he's got Becky for a friend.

'You're it!' she says, and the two of them laugh as she runs off. Tom chases after her, but she's far too fast, and the place is so big that soon she could be anywhere. Alongside him, I can see there's a smile on his face as he's looking for her. He runs around the entrance building, through the IT block, across the field, only getting occasional glimpses of her as she whizzes around the corners. 'Go get her, Tom!' I yell. I know he'll be panting like a dog by the time he catches Becky and it makes me laugh to think about it. He winds up behind the pavilion, where Danny Braithwaite's smoking a cig.

'What do you want, faggot?' he says.

'Nothing.' Tom can barely get the word out. His eyes are fixed on the cig. Danny notices this and approaches Tom. There's about four inches in height between the two, and a couple of years as well. Danny marches dead close to him and gives him a harsh look.

'You tell anyone about this and I'll fucking kill you,' he says. Tom's shaking in fear.

'Yes,' he says, and Danny gives him one last push before pointing for him to walk away. Tom's head hits the fence and he obliges. He cries, and soon Becky finds him.

'What's up?' she asks. Tom doesn't say anything. Just starts rubbing his head. Becky's far from understanding. 'You want me to be it for a bit?' She runs off.

'Why didn't you tell her?' I ask.

'I couldn't. Danny'd get me,' he says. The tears are running hard now. He wipes his face with his sleeve and runs off.

Becky soon catches him, but he doesn't care.

When Tom gets home, his mother's solemn. Sat on the couch, staring blindly at the telly with a face like a smacked arse. Tom walks way past her before she acknowledges him.

'How was school?' she says.

'Good,' he replies. 'Is there anything for tea?'

'Can't you make something yourself?'

'I don't know how.'

'Just put the oven on.'

Tom does this and puts some chips in, but WonderMother doesn't tell him to set a temperature, and twenty minutes later, when he takes them out and eats one, he gags it back up and throws it up onto the plate.

'Why didn't you set the temperature?' his mother asks.

'I didn't know,' he says. At this point his mother's phone vibrates. She picks it up and reads. It's his dad calling. She twists the temperature knob and tells Tom to put the chips back in again, and runs upstairs. We hear a faint but excited 'Harry, hi!'

before the footsteps drown her, and Tom is left alone to watch the oven. I want to tell him that he should ask her to help more, but every time he does, his dad gets in the way one way or another. I've never seen the guy, but his mother's hell bent on the two of them getting back together, so any chance at seeing or speaking to him has priority over Tom. This time round Tom manages to have a plate of chips that are almost cooked. He feels sick that night.

Bread again in the morning. I tell him to butter it. 'I can't do it for you,' I say. He heads to the fridge and mother gets it out for him. 'Let me do that for you, Tom,' she says before making a quick job of a better breakfast. 'Your father's coming over in a few days,' she adds.

'Good morning to you too, bitch,' I say.

'I want you to be good when he's over, okay?'

Tom nods, and mother follows up with 'Good.' She then gets up and walks into the kitchen, checks her phone, mutters to herself and paces around.

When we leave for school, his mother gives him a hug, tells him to have fun, and waits for us to step out of the house before returning the phone straight to her ear, and we walk on.

At lunch I make him buy something substantial. A sandwich from a small shop not far away. When we walk back to the playground, Jack and Danny are there.

'Tom!' says Jack. Tom gives them the slightest glance.

'Just keep walking, Tom,' I say. I put my arm around him, but he's not feeling any of it. He looks back at them again. He's scared, but there's also something else.

'Hey, Tom. Why are you ignoring us? Come here,' says Jack. The two start marching towards him. 'Don't turn your back on us, mate. We'll fucking have you.' He pushes Tom in the back, and Tom stumbles, but keeps on his feet and carries on walking. Danny runs up and grabs Tom's arm, swivels him round, and pushes him again. Tom falls flat on his back. He instantly gets back up, and looks to the sandwich that has gone places. He stands straight. Danny and Jack stand over to him.

'You gonna tell that Danny was smoking?' says Jack. 'Are you, you little shit? You're the kind who'll do that, aren't you?'

'No,' says Tom. 'I told him I wouldn't tell.' Jack pushes him again.

'I swear to God, if you tell, we'll beat the shit out of you.'

'Stop it!' At this, Tom reaches into his coat pocket and swings out a knife. He holds it to their faces. 'Go away!' he screams.

Where the fuck has he gotten that? 'Tom, listen,' I say. 'Put that down, now.' He has no intention of using it. He wants to scare them, but he's looking away from them now and Danny hits him square in the cheek. Jack, who had a look of fear on him, charges straight into Tom and brings him to the floor. People from around have started to notice this. Becky gets there first, but Danny holds her back, leaving Jack to pile into Tom.

'Let go of him,' she says. They don't reply. 'Get off him, Jack!' She sees the knife and starts wailing and wrestling with Danny. A few teachers run over, but before they even get close, Jack's left Tom with a nosebleed and plenty of bruises.

The knife was behind the three of them when Jack and Tom were finally pulled off each other, so the head teacher doesn't know whether to believe Jack and Danny's insistence that it was Tom's or not. The three of them get suspended for a week.

Back home, Tom's mother's frantic.

'If your father had been here, this never would've happened. Jesus, Tom, what were you thinking?'

'I don't know,' he says. Tom's just as confused as his mother, who's patched him up. A plaster here and there, a piece of toilet roll up each nostril. She hugs him. 'If your father was here,' she says, 'You never would've done this. You'd be a disciplined son, someone I could rely on.' Her mind then flutters away. 'Your father was a good man. I wish he'd never left. I wish ... but things'll be so much better when he comes back.' Tom hasn't seen his dad in seven years. Doesn't know what he looks like. Crazy bitch. Seven years ago Dad decided he'd had enough and bailed. That's when I first met Tom, when he was just a sprog. I imagine Dad was tired of the responsibility of fatherhood, or maybe Tom's mother was just as self-indulgent as she is now, and it drove him round the bend. Either way, from what Tom's told me, the conversation involved Dad saying that he needs to focus on his career, that he didn't think he was ready to be a dad or some shit. He must've been a workaholic, while she must've been the eight-year-old drama queen with fairy-tale fantasies that she still is today. I assume Mother's playing the your-son-needs-you card to lure him back.

She lets go. 'Don't you dare do anything like this when he arrives.' She checks her phone again, and Tom retreats to his bedroom.

'Are you okay?' I ask.

'I'm fine,' he says, getting into bed.

'Becky might come and see you, you know.'

'No, she won't.'

'Yes, she will. She's your friend.'

He keeps quiet.

'Look.' I know what he wants to hear. 'You're better than them, we both know that. They're arseholes.' Tom giggles at this. I ruffle his hair. 'They're not going nowhere in life. They're just picking on you because ...'

'Because what?'

'I don't know why, but you can't let them get to you. The ones like Becky, they're the ones you want to stick with.'

'And you. I want to stick around you too.'

I don't reply to this. Not an awful lot I could say, but it's when he says things like that that makes me glad that he's got someone like Becky. His mother comes in and sets a tray on the floor without saying a word and leaves. There's a burger, and plate of warm chips. I leave him to it.

I don't see him again for another couple of days. He's in his bedroom. It's the evening. He's reading a book, but he's lost focus and that's why I'm here.

'Guess who came?' he says. I shrug, and he looks at me. 'Becky.'

'Told you,' I say. He's got this bright boyish look on his face. His voice is giddy.

'She came over yesterday and we hung out all day. She said she hates Jack and Danny like I do, and she said I can come over whenever I want.'

Tom's mother suddenly walks through the door.

'Tom?' she says, 'who are you talking to?'

'No one,' says Tom. He blushes in embarrassment. Mother stands there, eyeing him up.

'You should be out playing, Tom. You won't have many friends if you're shut up in your room all day.' Tom reminds her that everyone else is at school, and she ignores this and leaves.

'She doesn't know I don't have many friends. She thinks I'm popular.'

'She wants to be popular herself, Tom,' I say. 'When's Dad gonna be here?'

'Tomorrow.'

There's another knock at the door. We hear Mother greet Becky, and Tom smiles at me.

The next morning, Tom tells me how they went to the park. How Becky had apologized for not getting Jack off him, and how she knows he didn't bring the knife to school. How they'd played on the swings and how they'd held hands on the climbing frame, and that Tom really liked it. He's grinning stupidly the whole time. He's smiling so much, it's as if he's got lockjaw.

'Tom!' Mother calls. 'Down here.'

Tom's smile fades slightly. He doesn't want to see his dad, or his mother. He wants to see Becky again, and wishes he had a phone like his mother now. Downstairs, his mother's dressed in a white and pink summer dress that covers just under her knees, and her light hazel hair has been curled, and reaches just to the tips of her shoulders.

'What do you think?' she says, twirling and spinning like a fluorescent model-wannabe. Tom just stares, not knowing what to think. There's a knock at the door. Mother dashes to the front door, runs her hands through her hair once more, and opens the door, beaming.

'Harry, hey,' she says. Dad walks in and they embrace. Dad's wearing a regular blue and white office shirt and casual black trousers. He's got short, dark hair and wears a nervous expression. They walk into the living room together.

'Tom, this is your dad,' she says. The cartoon smiling doesn't stop. 'Say hi.'

Tom doesn't say a thing, and his mother tells the two of them that she'll be back, and rushes upstairs. Dad walks up to Tom, and gets down on his level, ruffles his hair and smiles awkwardly.

'Hey sport,' he says. Tom stares at him in silence before Dad offers to sit down and watch telly. 'How's school?'

'It's okay,' Tom says.

Tom's mother eventually comes down with her handbag and motions for Dad that they should leave. 'I'll see you later,' Dad says. Tom remains silent, and Dad turns back to his son and his mouth opens slightly but no words come out. His mother's barely noticed by either of them, so she interjects. She grabs Dad's hand. 'Well,' she says. 'Shall we get going?' In the confusion, Dad allows himself to be carried away. 'You'll be okay while we're out, won't you Tom?' his mother quickly says.

Tom nods and the parents leave; his mother's in more of a hurry to get out the door than Dad is.

For the next few hours we talk. Tom thinks mostly about Becky, but he gives insight to the recent events.

'I'm sorry,' he says.

'What for?'

Tom sits quiet for a while. 'You know ...'

'Tom, I'll say it again. You're better than them. Don't you dare sink down to their level.' He takes a bite out of the lunch he's made and starts to sob.

'I'm sorry. I want just want them to stop.'

'I know.' I hug the kid. Bless him.

The next day, we sit in the front room again, and Tom starts to think about Becky.

'Reckon she'll call again?' I say.

'I hope so,' he says. There's plenty of uncertainty in his voice. He makes a sandwich and watches TV. It dawns on me that Tom's barely been punished for what happened with Jack and Danny. Just a scolding. I get an idea. School's been over for a while now.

'Why don't you call on her this time?'

'Huh?'

'Why do you have to wait for her?'

Tom looks at me for a while, as if I've asked him to do the impossible.

'She'll like it. Promise.' I smile at him for that extra encouragement, and he gets giddy. He puts on his trainers, and marches out.

'What should I ask her?'

'Just ask if she wants to come out. Ask if she wants to go to the park or something. Hell, she might even invite you inside.'

He blushes at the thought of this.

We're about half a mile away from her street when we hear a familiar voice.

'Tom. Tom, you piece of shit. Get over here, now!'

'Shit,' I mutter. We turn. It's Jack and Danny. We pace backwards, but they've already started running. 'Tom, run!'

He sprints away, as fast as he can towards Becky's street but it's no use. They catch up to him in seconds. Danny trips him. Tom cries out in pain.

'You got a knife on you now, have you?' says Jack. 'Gonna stab us, are you?' Danny's kicking Tom in the stomach over and over and Jack joins in, but he goes one further and kicks him in his face. I try to get in the way, but there's nothing I can do.

'Hey!' we hear. 'Get off him!'

It's Becky. She approaches the three of them. Danny walks aggressively over to her, and like he did before, he holds her back. Jack stops hitting Tom and kneels down.

'Don't you ever think you can hurt us, mate. You think you're tough bringing in a knife like that?'

Tom whimpers in pain. Becky's screaming makes me wish I could do anything more than just watch. Why the fuck isn't Dad around? Why the fuck has the man left Tom with that useless shit-for-brains mother? I stand there in frustration. Tom can barely yell out in pain. Becky screams one last time.

'Get off him, Jack. Get off him and leave him alone!'

In the midst of all this, Tom isn't thinking enviously. He isn't fantasising about bringing them to their knees and witnessing them plead for forgiveness. He's thinking about Dad, and how maybe one day he'll put up with all of his mother's weirdness and come live with them. He's hoping that Dad will one day teach him how to fish and how to fix cars. As Tom goes silent, he isn't wondering where his dad has been the past seven years, though one day he'll ask. He's wondering if he could have spent seven years protecting him. Or maybe that's what I'm wondering.

We can hear Becky's screaming fade. Jack's let go, and he and Danny leave. Tom's completely beaten, not even making an attempt to move. Becky uses her phone to call her parents.

'Tom,' I say. 'Tom, mate, get up!'

I grab his hand.

'Dad,' I hear him say. His eyes are barely open.

'That's right, Tom. It's Dad.'

'Dad,' he says again. Becky tries to lift him up, but he collapses back on the ground. He goes completely silent and I realise then. I'm not his dad. I'm not someone who can lift him up. Dad could take a bullet for him, something I can't do. And it's awful because Tom thinks I can. Becky cries in fear, and holds the same hand that I do.

The last time I ever see Tom is after Becky's parents get him home. His parents are already there, and his mother nearly keels over at the shock of seeing what state her son is in. Dad picks Tom up and carries him to bed, before ordering a cold flannel, bandages, and the like. Tom can barely keep his eyes open. His mother's screaming to call an ambulance, but Dad tells Becky's parents to keep her downstairs and to keep her calm while he takes care of Tom. Seeing how he strokes his hair and promises Tom that everything is going to be okay, while treating his wounds, I'm guessing that a father-son relationship is born here. Dad patches him up, and he stays with Tom quietly. Becky enters the room to see if he's okay. Dad says he's going to be fine. She holds Tom's arm. I think that Tom's glad that he has three people around him that he can rely on, and it says a lot that he can have seven bells of shit beaten out of him, and afterwards still smile. Mother's wailing has died down, and there's no sound up here either. Tom's eyes are closing, and Becky's asking if he's going to be okay. Dad says sure, but he needs rest. We hear Tom's mother's feet pounding up the stairs, and as she charges in, Dad is instantly by her side. Becky leaves. 'I'll come back tomorrow,' she says. Tom's parents acknowledge her as she leaves and they go to Tom's side.

'Is he going to be okay?' she asks.

'Let's just leave him be,' says Dad.

'Tom,' I say. 'Tom, you there mate?' He doesn't answer. He just moans quietly. I turn to his parents, and even though they can't hear me, I speak.

'You know what?' I say. 'I'm sick of you. I'm sick of everything Tom and I've had to go through since you left, Dad.'

Mother whispers to Dad: 'He needs you, Harry.'

Dad shakes his head. 'Karen ...'

I'm fuming at the pair of them. 'Tom,' I say. 'Tom ... Christ ...' What do I do?

Dad continues. 'I just need some time.'

Mother's practically begging. 'Just stay, Harry. Stay for us both. You don't know what it's like. You don't know what I've had to deal with.'

'Fucking "deal with",' I think. 'What example have you been going by? You let him suffer, you self-centred, inconsiderate bitch!' I swing for her. My hand wisps straight through her. 'He fucking needed you, Karen! Harry, say something!' None of this is right.

Mother carries on: 'Harry, he can't look after himself. He gets into trouble at school. I don't know what to tell him. You were always the one to comfort him back then. He needs a figure like you.'

'Why aren't you there for him?' Dad asks.

'I am.'

'Look at him, Karen. You're not.' I can't do anything. That's a hard, cold fact. I pray for Dad to do the right thing here. 'It's clear he's having troubles and you don't notice.'

'He doesn't talk, Harry.'

'That's because he has no one to talk to!'

'Just be here for us. Please.'

'Karen ...' Dad sighs. He knows just as well I do.

She reaches out for his hand, and he lets her take it. She looks at him, and there are tears down her face, but I don't believe her. But what do I know? Now there's a thought ...

They look at their son and for a second they seem like parents. I feel that I've shadowed the little'un for far too long now. And here he is. I don't speak. The three of us watch Tom peacefully, and Tom sleeps.

Ghosts are the least of the horrors in this new story
from Fiction Desk regular Matthew Licht ...

Washout

Matthew Licht

Bike clothes get whiffy fast. Bikes have their own individual stinks, especially the saddles. Not that I go around sniffing strange bike seats, but I wouldn't exactly have ruled it out, the way things were going.

Winter cycling conditions keep the stink in check, at least. The pong-wave that precedes and follows me in summer spreads animal panic, elicits extreme stink-eye from fellow two-wheel travellers. But I never felt like opening scarred financial veins for the latest Odor-o-No cycle gear, or going laundry-crazy on the old. One suit for warm weather, one for cold is good enough for trees and animals, therefore okay with me.

There was something wrong with this philosophy, but the problem only became obvious when the washing machine in the basement broke. I mean, when it broke beyond the point where Tony could fix it.

Despite his drug addiction, sexual hang-ups and obsessive/depressive behaviour-patterns, Tony retains an engineer's brain and is almost amazingly handy with tools, moving parts and circuit design. But the ancient USA-manufactured top-loader washing machine he found on the street became his Waterloo.

No sparks flew, no black or white smoke plumed, there was no final explosion. The only injury was to Tony's self-esteem. He kicked the washing machine, hard enough to hurt his foot, but not hard enough to give the dead contraption a miracle-jolt resuscitation.

'Bad news,' he said, when he emerged from the gloomy, mouldy, spiderweb-spangled basement. 'We got to find us another washing machine.'

Much worse news for me than Tony. The guy's a regular thrift store clothes-horse. Cheaper, he says, to get pre-ironed dry-cleaned shirts from the Salvation Army than to hit a regular haberdasher and shell out for new. Also a better deal in terms of irreplaceable time-outlay. Scavenged rags don't skeeve him. He even goes for used shoes. Socks, he says, are condoms for feet. Ditto, long underwear for the rest of the body. Mounds of unserviceably dirty used clothes lend Tony's room an even more subterranean, stalagmite-infested look.

Back when I still lived like a civilised human, I had me some clothes. Socks for every day of the week, maybe even a few pairs for emergencies. Underwear, ironed shirts, you name it. Then the sky fell, or the floor dropped, or whatever hit me happened. Nails, hammered by parties unknown into dank, unfamiliar walls, became where I hung jeans, shirt, sweater, jacket. Grim briefs and socks stashed in a cardboard box next to the scavenged mattress where I currently kennel. When I leave the cave, it's usually on a bike.

'Shit,' Tony said, as he wiped his hands on his pants, the bottom half of some dead penny-ante businessman's workwear, instead of washing them at the crowded, grease-saturated kitchen sink. 'Eerie coincidence: the minute you said "washing machine", I was hit with an urge to do industrial loads of laundry. Can't explain it, but the urge felt positive, like a kind of breakthrough.'

'Break through what?' Let's face it, *no clean clothes* doesn't top the list of Tony's personal problems, but he had a point. Got to start somewhere.

'Let me break something to you,' he said. 'I'm not the type who'll tell a grown man his business, but we live together, and, despite having had our differences ...'

Like trying to kill each other, for instance.

'... we're friends. So listen, my friend, you're starting to smell.'

The hideous baboon at the zoo tells his cage-mate she's ugly. The vomit-crusted hobo sprawled next to you on the drunk-tank floor vehemently recommends AA.

'Well I sweat a lot,' I said. 'On account of I try to stay healthy and fit, in mind and body. I prefer to think I stink vigorous, instead of ...' Tony existed in a scent-cloud of depression and death.

'Dude, you smell like piss.'

A silence fell, like the last nail had just sunk home on the pine box-top. Hadn't occurred to me I was already old. Miles don't pedal away years. 'Oh. Shit.'

Two men in a decrepit house filled with worn rubber tires and street junk stared at each other across the gulf between individual lives that had brought them together. Outside, the wind bullied loose snow and garbage. Not too far away, a river ran under a thick cover of ice. Everything outside the house smelled clean, if only due to extreme cold.

Maybe I've got a year or two on Tony, but at that moment he seemed an enviable teenager, minus hair and hope.

So that's why I can't get a date, or a job. That's why editors change their tone when I turn up at their offices. Lady editors in particular. Always wondered why they want to meet me in the first place.

'But I take showers,' I said. For some reason, I felt I had to plead my case. 'And I shave now and then ... and wash my clothes fairly often. I'm a clean person, honest.'

'Hey it happens, man. I can't explain it.'

Shit happens. Everyone says so. That piss happens is a more original concept. Piss, the perfume of unhappy old age.

'Let's go out and find another washing machine,' I said.

We were both beyond the human condition where, if you need some crucial appliance, commodity, or service, you go to the appropriate commercial place of business to obtain what's required. We'd devolved into nocturnal scavengers, on the order of shabbily dressed, unmasked, ungainly bipedal raccoons. Tony's car had long since been repossessed. I haven't owned an automobile since I lived in LA, in what seemed like another life.

People move on, change their habits and scenery, leave formerly necessary accoutrements behind, occasionally dispose of functional-but-outdated washing machines. Like, when they die.

Since we live in a rough, poor, mostly black neighbourhood, we dressed for the outing like North Pole Tuaregs, with nearly no white skin showing.

Nobody on the block was busy dragging still-functional washing machines out into the street.

We proceeded in silence. Caucasian voice-patterns arouse hostile vibes. The only dead giveaway was Tony's footwear. Blacks and black brogues / white socks don't mix. Tony's stuck in cop-shoe mode, something to do with two-for-one deals at a Times Square shoe shop that went out of business decades ago. We hugged walls, kept to the shadows, speeded up at intersections. We cased the laundromats first. Not many left. Chinese and Indians have taken over the business, speculating on ghetto moms who show off spotless designer diapers and drool-bibs. It didn't seem impossible that new laundromat management would invest in state-of-the-art machinery, dispose of the obsolete.

Yes Soap Radio was locked up tight, with a possible starved attack dog on patrol behind the prison-style roll-down gate. The alley behind the shop had nothing to show but disembowelled garbage sacks. It was over a mile to the next laundro-joint. Tony, unused to walking, claimed his cop-shoes were causing blisters, hammer-toes, bunions, chill-blains.

'Cowboy up,' I said. 'And prepare for heavy lifting, in case we get lucky.'

'Maybe we can hire a washer-woman who'll work for crack, or food, or something. We'll teach her how to cook ... and fuck.'

The idea packed massive appeal, out there in the wind and cold. Something else for me and Tony to fight about, unless we could locate two ghetto-bunny maid-slaves.

'Maybe we should get married,' I said. 'Some guys do, you know.'

Tony thought about it. He'd already been married, once. His wife took off with a Wall Street broker who knew, she said, everything there is to know about French wines. She used the plural. Wine was wine, where Tony and I came from. 'You're not really my type,' he said. 'And I don't think it's legal in Jersey, yet. And you can't iron shirts for shit. And you probably don't swallow.'

'Let's keep looking.'

Footsteps echo loud, on blocks where most of the doors and windows have been boarded up and X'ed out with recycled ply-lumber. Or at least the footsteps sounded like echoes, with the rhythm slightly off. Tony heard them too.

'Someone's following us,' he said.

'Don't look around. Shows fear.'

'Glocks shoot really, really straight,' he said, a little too loud, I thought, for someone who was in fact strapping self-defence artillery. 'Hammered nails for an hour with mine yesterday, and still hit bullseyes every shot.' We stopped to discuss handgun factoids and risk a look around.

The entire point of following someone is usually not to let the people you're following know you're following them. No menacing shapes leapt from the darkness to announce, hey sorry okay I admit I was tailing you but I'll cut it out now since you're obviously on to me. But someone was there.

Tony felt the non-reassuring presence too. 'Now I know,' he whispered, 'how those poor little pronghorn goats feel when they're left out as tied-up tiger bait in Indian mangrove forests.'

We kept walking, entered a tunnel of brick wall and heavy-duty chain-link fence.

Overflowing dumpsters hunkered down like obese witches behind the Salvation Army warehouse hard by the long-abandoned Erie-Lackawanna Railroad marshalling yard. Mercury light made the dirty-brick building look like a hell-within-hell San Quentin for the particularly punishment-worthy damned. A freight train somewhere in the New Jersey night let out a lonesome tri-tone howl.

'Oh this is a really good place,' Tony said. He sounded like a suburban high school girl entering her first black-neighbourhood juke joint. All her Pop's stern warnings poofed into garbage-incinerator smoke, annihilated by music that made humans dance and sweat together, regardless of such silly non-considerations as skin colour and economic status. 'People drop off their stuff near the dumpsters rather than lug it upstairs. I found a McIntosh amp with only three tubes burnt out, a pair of cordovan wingtips only half a size too big, a black cashmere scarf with nary a moth-'ole, pornographic Meissen figurines, full set of Playboy from 1965 to 1969 ...' He probably would've gone on all the nightmarish night.

'Washing machine, motherfucker. Remember, we're supposed to be scavenging for a washing machine.'

'Oh yeah, and once I found a genuine Ray-O-Vac robot housewife model. Got a wino to help me load her into the Mercedes ...' Tony waxed wistful about the car he almost never drove and on which he even more seldom paid instalments until it, too, was taken away from his life and made to vanish. 'Probably still in the basement, back towards the furnace somewhere, with my wife's hypothetical sculpture retrospective.' He still said wife, not ex-wife. 'Right next to all the other washing machines I found, or bought, or couldn't get myself to let go of ...'

'Satan says he likes living in your washing machine collection, Tony. He feeds on the Thanksgiving leftovers you can't bear to jettison.'

'Hey, what am I supposed to do if barbecued popes' noses taste so damn good even years after ... Listen, I just heard it again. Something huge is shadowing us.'

Strange sounds, like a phosphorescent elephant attempting to silently slither between a brick wall and garbage containers.

Electrified concertina-wound razor-wire festoons atop the railway yard's chain-link fence perimeter were the only possible way out of whatever occult trouble me and Tony were in. A flying, pole-free pole-vault, a few minutes of slashing, thrashing, flashing, gory Laocoön writhing, then the lovely permanent darkness would descend, like an immense, amorphous ink-stain of bats and manta rays.

Hoping for a glimpse of the stalking behemoth, I spotted exactly what we were looking for, i.e. a heavy-duty front-load washer-dryer combo. White enamelled one-eyed giant twins, forlorn relics from an orphanage driven out of business by adoption-crazed infertile Yuppie hordes, absolutely too huge to be scavenged, unless there was also an abandoned Sikorsky UH-235 Sky-Crane helicopter nearby. But we'd probably run out of chopper-fuel and crash, half an ironic mile from the defunct Heavenly Rest Hospital in Squeehonken. Firemen would hose our human Char-B-Q cinders down sewer drains forged in the extinguished furnaces of nearby Harrison. Tabloid headlines would run along the lines of, 'Ghosts / Aliens / Jersey Devil Heli-Hi-Jack Disaster!', except the Metuchen Monitor don't print no more.

'Check it out, Tony. Ray-O-Vac, your favourite freakin' US Gov't contractor home appliance brand. War Pigs gonna wash away our pit- and shit-stains.'

'Wow hey will you look at that?' Tony approached the presumed-dead machines with respectful apprehension, as though they might be unexploded bombs in tempting shape. He couldn't resist buffing their cold black staring portholes with his sleeve. 'Coin-op ignition can be easily hot-wired, and I can probably rig the dryer to run on furnace-exhaust, or off that absurd fucking pottery kiln Barbara swore up and down would get her into the Museum of Modern Art's permanent collection.' Barbara was the ex-wife Tony refused or was unable to ex out of his dreams. Yet another problem we have in common. I can't shake dreams of happy togetherness with the lady I left in the Big City. Also can't help wondering if she still dreams about me. Or is nightmare a verb too?

The next frightening noise was like an endless breath.

The moon burned through low cloud cover to shine on Tony, further fondling machinery left over from Big America's gleaming high-standard-of-living dreams. Cold beams spotlighted a Harris Tweed raglan sleeve waving seductively from a closed, shredded steamer trunk. Hello, scavenging sailor. Right this way for dumpster-dandy wardrobe supplementation. Colourful cashmere sweaters, college scarves, military-cut tartan trousers are stored within. Fuck your usual dirty bike-monk get-up. Like a zombie, I approached.

A corpse flopped from the trunk with a muffled bass-drum thump, followed by an incredible stink-wave that out-wrestled the cold. Dead bald guy stared open-mouthed at the night sky, big sad yellow teeth and a hoof-print dent in his forehead, as though some rabid mule had scored a bullseye to his brain. Black blood-crusts in his hairy ears. Not the world's greatest shaver, while he was still alive. Defensive wounds on his hands, ribs obviously stove in, legs twisted at horrible crashed-puppet angles.

But I didn't shit my pants. I pissed them instead.

Tony was shaken from laundry dreams by the stink of urine and decomp. He shambled over, gawked, sucked in wind and barfed his Lonely Man / Hungry Man TV dinner all over the defenceless dead guy. Somehow, he managed not to get puke on himself, so he was two cleanliness-steps ahead of me.

With an increasingly cold crotch, I tossed the steamer trunk coffin for spare pants, but there weren't any. Just a tweed coat. The dead guy, whoever he was, was dressed in frayed long johns, but they didn't seem like a good substitute for my soiled duds. Increasingly desperate and ashamed, I dived into the Salvation Army's yellow clothes-disposal bin precisely in the manner the red stick-figure sign warned clothes-hungry illegal immigrant stowaways from the nearby harbour not to, unless they wanted to be crushed and suffocated.

But the risk paid off, in spades. Found a serviceable pair of severely off-white canvas janitor pants. Pulled off my shoes.

The piss and puke hadn't reached my ragg-wool hiking socks yet. Excellent. Stripped off pants, wiped down legs, discarded the pissed, worn-out jeans I would soon have had to toss anyway but I hate throwing out clothes just because they've developed holes.

Tony saw me strip off my ruined pants. 'Jesus,' he said. 'You gonna dance around naked now? Think bald white guy voodoo's gonna make this poor mook come back alive and tell us who killed him when it's obvious we're next?'

He had a point. I pulled on the janitor pants in a hot flash and rummaged for potential weapons. Liberally strewn bottles were too shattered. Reinforcement-bar discards were too long and heavy for use as cudgels or spears. No kitchen knives or cleavers nowhere.

'Why don't we just use this?' Tony said, and whipped an ugly squared-off 9mm automatic from his waistband. 'Freakin' phenomenal stopping power. At least that's what it said on the box.'

'The box said "freakin' phenomenal"?'

He shot a slow burn while invisible demons of the night besieged and menaced us. The Salvation Army monster, at least, wasn't fucking around. Got to watch out, when scavenging. Sometimes you find something good among the junk. Sometimes something bad among the junk finds you. We'd found what we were looking for, but cleanliness of such a massive order as the cyclopean Ray-O-Vac washer-dryer twins promised was way beyond our grasp.

No way to tell what the dead guy was scrounging for when whatever got him got him, but he paid the supreme price for being old, cheap, and useless.

The gory crushed corpse rustled. I nearly split from my skin like a man-sized cicada. The Salvation rat-Army must've been sniffing around the decomposing stiff stuffed in the steamer trunk for days. Slavering rodents wanted in on the suddenly available feast. The dead guy still had most of his face, crunched as it was. The rats were going to eat it.

'Shoot him, Tony.'

'What for? Dude's already dead. He won't bother us none.'

'Shoot him so the friggin' rats'll scatter. I hate rats.'

'Well I ain't crazy about 'em neither, but if I shoot we'll have bigger problems ... like pigs.'

'The pigs could eat the rats.'

'Dipshit, I meant pigs as in police.'

'Pigs wouldn't be a problem, in this case. They'd get us outta here.'

'Yeah, to a nice cosy cell full of giant two-legged black doped-up rats who rape pretty little white guys like you and me.'

'We don't got to worry about that. Nobody wants to rape our ass no more, Tony. Let's face it. We're old. We're ugly. We're safe.'

Tony was miffed. 'Speak for yourself. Anyway, I ain't going to prison. Promised my mama. And I don't waste bullets on harmless shadows.'

The corpse started up a furious shuffling spaz-dance. Rats were having a ball with him, but discreetly. No rats visible, no rat-squeaks audible. It was too horrible to watch. Big brave hero that I am, I gave the dancing dead guy a kick.

Wasn't bad enough a dead carcass was doing the anti-rigor-mortis Watusi, he had to start singing.

'Oh pleeeeeeease, don't kick me 'round no more.

You seeeeeeee, I been kicked a-round before.

Kick my heart like a can,

How much pain can I staaaaaand?'

The question went unanswered. Incredibly, the dead man's lips hadn't moved. The rats either stopped disturbing the remains, or whichever sinister ventriloquist puppeteer had manipulated his un-mummified limbs dropped the strings.

Heavy silence, as the shadows of the junked streetscape oozed together into a black pterodactyl that levitated, became one with the clouds and doused the moon.

Tony re-holstered his gun in his waistband.

The dead guy had gone back to being resolutely dead. That was his job, now.

'Okay ... we were looking for a washing machine. We found a washing machine, a serendipitous dryer, and a dead body. Only, we can't budge the laundry equipment 'cause we ain't got no truck. We probably shouldn't move the stiff, neither, since what we got here is a possible crime scene. Think we ought to call the po-lice?'

'Think they'd give us a hand with the washer-dryer? Cops might just understand a couple of dirty guys who want to come clean ... I mean, who want to get clean.'

The white enamel machines considered us with outsized beady cyclopean eyes. They had no mouths with which to mock us, no noses to take in the tang of fear, no ears to hear our inane attempts at logic.

No point calling the cops. Reporting dead bodies only leads to nosy questions and unnecessary paperwork, besides which, neither of us had a cell phone. Tony had one once, but it ceased to function during the course of one of our domestic dust-ups. There were no phonebooths around, and even if there had been, the telephones inside them would no doubt not be in working order. I grabbed the Harris Tweed overcoat off its hanger in the steamer trunk, resisted the urge to try it on for a possible fit, draped it over the corpse. No protection against rats, roaches, or earwigs. A cloak of dignity, nothing more. The dead shouldn't be forced to dance or sing by unseen forces.

'Salvation Army workers will find him in the morning. At least we put the poor bastard in a position to be found. We've done our bit, so let's blow. Where'd you get that pistol, anyway?'

'They were having a clearance sale at the mall. The old guy believed me when I said I was a cop on vacation from Nevada.'

'Is there a warehouse-type department store in this guns n' ammo shopping mall of yours?'

'Uh yeah, I think they got one of those.'

'Okay. Look man, I know this will seem outlandish, but tomorrow you and me are going to go to that department store and we shall head to the home appliance department and purchase ourselves a washing machine and a dryer and we will make arrangements for skilled licensed technicians to deliver and install the aforementioned machines in our place of residence. Maybe they'll also agree to remove the busted, twisted wreckage that is a freaking travesty of how grown men ought to take care of themselves ... if we hand them perhaps a measly ten dollars, each. This is how normal people operate.'

'How would you know how normal people operate? You practically live on a bicycle. You're like a nomad who ain't even got basic, primitive nomad survival skills.'

'Once, I was normal. So were you. Think back, think hard. The memories are there. Clean clothes isn't too big a step for mankind. But we got to be willing to take that step.'

The giant pale Ray-O-Vac twins mutely whispered, 'You'll never make it.'

But we did. And while we were at it, in Shopping Mall Appliance Land, I filled out an application for a position in the department store's warehouse. When the nice lab-coated manager asked if I knew how to operate a forklift, I told him I put in two freakin' years on a payload forklift at the Da Nang air base. The way he shook my hand told me I got the job.

As soon as we were out in the parking lot, where no parked car awaited us, Tony smacked his forehead.

'We done threw away our dough,' he said.

'Huh? How?'

'There's gotta be some way we can hijack your forklift out of the mall when you're on the night shift and we'll go get them Ray-O-Vacs. C'mon, let's go back in and nix that freaky contract we just signed.'

'Forget it, Tony. Those clean-robots weren't meant for us. Think of this deal as, we're headed back to human.'

But we returned to the grim dead-end alley to check anyway. While it was still light out.

The machines and the dead guy were gone. Felt like whatever had shadowed us was no longer there either. But maybe that was just because the winter sun was shining cold.

Tony whipped out his Glock and we took turns blasting away at rats and, more successfully, stationary discarded objects.

'So, you was in the 'Nam?' he asked.

'You fuckin' kidding me?'

Parting is such sweet sorrow in this new story from Jason Atkinson ... especially if you don't know what to do with the part you're left with.

Half Mom

Jason Atkinson

Mom arrived UPS with little fanfare. Just a 'Sign here, ma'am,' and a curt 'Have a good day,' and off to the races, another brown box in an endless line of brown boxes, another human life keeping the engine of commerce in motion while the earth orbited the sun. Clara reached out, took her mom in her arms and let the apartment slam shut. She felt her mom in her hands and thought about how in moments such as these, when one receives a dead mother in a cardboard box, life can be seen with a greater clarity.

This was her apartment.

The sun was shining.

The dishes in the sink needed to be washed.

There was a table across the room.

Clara unpacked Mom and placed her on the table. The urn was absent decorations: no lounging Greek bodies eating grapes, no fucking and hunting. No chaise. Just cold metal. It could have doubled as a travelling coffee mug. Her father, fulfilling a deep-seated need to label things, had taped a picture of her mother onto the side of the urn. On the picture he wrote 'Mom,' just in case Clara might forget.

He had sent her a text:

Sending Mom to you. Should arrive tomorrow. xo.

There was no plan for Mom's ashes. No final resting place. No special ceremony. Her death, now almost six months in the past, had started to recede into a stupid memory. She missed the moment when her mother died. She missed the rawness of that, the immediacy of the loss. She longed for those early tears, when she would just pour out at the wrong times: social events where no one likes to speak of death, and vegetable aisles where you check for ripe avocado.

'Are you okay, dear?'

'Fine, thank you.'

She was fine. And getting finer. Finetabulous thank you very much, and she could control things now, except for nights where she would jolt awake at night and cry and cry and cry.

No plans.

No plan to scatter her ashes in the ocean or into a river or inside the soil of a garden, turn Mom into a carrot. Part of this was Mom's fault: she had never communicated where she might like her ashes scattered. Just an 'I want you to cremate me,' periodic command peppered throughout the course of her life.

'Just make sure to cremate me,' she said after waiting three hours in the Small World line at Disney World.

'We know, Mom,' Clara said.

'Yes,' said Dad, trying to make light, 'But where do you want us to scatter your ashes, dear?'

'Anywhere but here.' She always said these things in a way that made Clara laugh, but then later feel very sad.

Where would they scatter her?

There was a note in the box.

'Dear Clara. Please enjoy your mother and keep her in a safe place. I have only sent half of her. I'm sure it will be fine.'

'I have only set half of her.'

Massive WTF rage out into the farthest cosmos. Clara reached for the text messaging function on her phone.

wtf dad? Half mom?

Sry xo

are you crazy??!

call me

She called him. When she called him it meant serious shit.

'What were you thinking?' she said.

'I'm sorry, honey. Are you uncomfortable with this?'

'Dad, it's borderline psychotic.'

A silence.

'Then tell me where we should spread Mom's ashes.'

'I don't know.'

'We need to make a decision.'

'Yes. I know. But I don't think Mom would want this. She wouldn't want to halved, Dad. For Christ's sake.'

'Okay. Fine. If you don't like it, if it doesn't give you comfort, you can send her back and we'll, I don't know, we'll put her in the backyard garden. How about that?'

'No. Not there. She hated gardening.'

'Then I don't know, Clara. See, this is this problem. Until you decide where we can put her ... you, I don't know, you have to live with her. Some of her.'

Pressure tactics.

'What about your half?' she said.

'Don't worry about my half.'

'Did you buy another urn?'

'No. But I will.'

'Then where is she?'

'I just put her in an old soda bottle for right now.'

'What?!'

'Grapefruit soda. She liked that stuff.'

'Dad!! WHAT are you ...'

'I'm kidding, Clara. Can you please try and relax?' said Dad.

Clara rolled her eyes, as if those things could be heard over the phone.

Half a person is a difficult thing for the mind to contemplate.

There are so many questions. Did she get the lower body or upper body? If she had a choice she would want the upper body of course, but if she had to content herself with the lower body, she could manage that too. But what if she had got only the left side? Would she prefer the left side over the right side?

She marvelled at how long her mind allowed itself to think in this manner. It took half a bottle of wine for her to realise that she had just got a bunch of random bits of her mom. A mish mash o' mom. Bits of her mom and coffin and cremation bag or god knows what else they burn you in. Weird chemicals and residue from other people who have been burnt in the same cremation chamber.

'Jesus,' she thought as she finished that bottle and opened another.

If her mother were to form before her, were to rise out of the urn like a genie, it would no doubt be a strange, alien sight. A disembodied floating half-human. Part of a leg, a few teeth. A section of the spine.

'What have you donnne with meeee child,' she would intone.

'It was Dad's fault,' Clara would say.

The disembodied half-Mom ghost would then go into the kitchen, pour itself a grapefruit soda, and wonder aloud about Clara's prospect for marriage, a better job, and children. Clara would tell her that she was twenty-eight, and that she lived in New York City, and that she just wanted to have fun. Because that's what girls do.

'Twenty-nine is not that yoooouunngg, Clara.'

This fantasy made Clara sweat.

She couldn't have an urn sitting around the house at her age. What sort of signal would it send a prospective mate if she had half a mom sitting on her mantle? She could imagine the conversation:

PROSPECTIVE BREEDING PARTNER: What's this?

CLARA: It's an urn that contains the ashes of my mother. But only half, as my father insisted on keeping some of it.

(Sounds of potential mate running away.)

She texted Dad again.

I'm putting mom in closet.
If that's what u want honey i'm happy xo
what do you mean 'if that's what you want'
i'm happy if u are happy xo
why do you keep saying xo...that's mom's thing
Sry
just stop using xo
okay. Sry
and can you fully spell out words, dad?
Sorry. Which closet will you put her in?

The high closet. The storage closet, the remote closet. In a box in that high storage closet, the highest closet, way at the back. In the box with the lock where she would never have to look at half Mom except in moments when she really wanted to commiserate with her.

'I got married, Mom.'

'I have a good job.'

'I have children.'

'My children are married.'

'I'm dead now. Where are you?'

Clara would put her in The Lock Box.

The best part of her plan was that The Lock Box was fireproof. Half Mom would be safe there and there would be plenty of room as The Lock Box only contained documents like Clara's birth certificate and her social security card and some leftover marijuana that an ex-boyfriend forgot about. Were her apartment to burn down, she would triumphantly pull her mom's ashes out of the ashes, out of the rubble. She would be a good daughter.

'Thank you for saving meee,' Mom would intone into her ear.

Unfortunately, Half Mom did not completely fit inside The Lock Box, rendering The Lock Box unlockable. Half Mom only almost fit and so the key only almost locked. Clara pushed and pulled and prodded on the box and eventually broke the fragile key in half, rendering The Lock Box now truly and utterly until the end of time unlockable.

'Well, my apartment is probably not going to burn down,' she thought.

A small voice at the back of her mind then spoke.

'Here is a case,' it said, 'where things are going wrong, and, if yours were a voice more attuned to the mysteries of the universe, to the vicissitudes of life, it would notice this and maybe consider that your mother might not want to be going into a lockbox.'

She considered this, very deeply considered this.

She chose to ignore it.

Instead she just closed The Broken Lock Box and crudely taped it with some grey duct tape. It was better to just get this out of the way for now and, at an time when she was feeling a little more clear-headed, she would purchase a better, bigger larger Lock Box that could comfortably contain all her important documents and Half Mom.

She climbed up to the high closet, eager to shove The Desecrated Lock Box deep inside and move on with her life. The Formerly Lock Box, now not fully closed, would not slide into the place it had previously occupied. Again, the small voice.

'Don't put Mom in the closet in a crudely duct-taped box. It's disrespectful.'

Again, she ignored it.

As she shoved the The Crudely Duct-taped Lock Box into the too narrow space it seemed as if the world got very angry. The sound of the avenue outside of her window was ferocious. The sound of accumulated metal passing by, mostly trucks, and then the angry sirens of police vehicles and the ambulance. It felt overwhelming, as if the world was shouting out her.

She pushed on Half Mom.

'Get. In. There,' she shouted.

The Lock Box, Half Mom within, then slipped from her fingers.

It fell to the ground.

'Fuck!' she shouted, it was an extended 'fuck,' one that rang as an accompaniment to the falling box, which hit hard enough to dislodge the duct tape, and allow its contents, including Half Mom, to spill all over the floor.

Half Mom spilled open, spreading grey ash into the air.

'Shit, shit, shit,' she thought, and she jumped down from the ladder. She bent down to clean Mom up, but as she began to breathe her in, and got the odour of her, she stood up. Her head throbbed. Mom smelled like a crater on the moon. Mom looked like the moon. Mom's photograph, still taped to the side of urn, lay face up, collected tiny ash particles.

There was no best way to get all the ash back in the urn; she just ended up scooping it with her fingers. She wet a paper towel and cleaned the floor. Unsure of what to do with a moist paper towel infused with Mom ash, she just decided to stuff the paper inside the urn, too. Then she scraped off her fingers over the urn, leaving Mom residue on the side of the urn as a bartender might do with salt.

She went to the sink and grabbed the soap. She had to clean the Mom off her hands.

Here she paused.

'If I wash her off like this, I'm sending Mom to the sewer,' she thought.

She began to lick her fingers, cleaning Mom off this way. It tasted strange, but for some reason felt right. She thought of tiny mother birds regurgitating food for their babies.

'When you were a baby,' her mother once said, 'I used to sometimes chew up your food and put it in your mouth. I don't know why I did that. I think I was just scared. Scared I would lose you.'

Clara licked every bit of her mother off of her hands.

She let Mom be after that.

She threw herself down on the bed, and sleep settled on top of her.

She allowed her eyes to slowly close. In every bedtime there was that moment where she had to relinquish control, where she had to depart and go down the drain of sleep. She could feel herself drifting away, just about to drop into the hole of sleep. To go beneath the ocean of sleep. To let the wave of sleep crash over her and block out all of the sensory impressions of life. Right at the moment when sleep was going to roll over, right at the millisecond when sleep was supposed to happen, she froze up, and began to think, began to worry.

'I am afraid,' she thought.

She sat up.

'Clara.'

'Mom?'

She looked out into the dark.

'Mom,' she said.

She saw it all rise up, in all of its grey ashen blackness, and hover over her. Before the moment could be fully hammered out, before time could be completely taken in, it plunged inside of her, sliding into her skin, wrapping itself around her.

are you there?

I'm here xo

One of the scariest things about ghosts is that they aren't always fair. You don't have to plunder a tomb to unleash something horrible on yourself: sometimes all it takes is a little curiosity, or finding yourself by chance in a bedroom with unusual curtains. And sometimes all it takes is a little kindness ...

No Good Deed

Amanda Mason

Like the rest of us on the bus, the old lady is soaked to the skin. She's wearing a dark shapeless coat, a black felt hat, and a long ragged grey scarf. Her shopping trolley, a grubby red tartan thing, bulging and torn in places, blocks the aisle. The bus swings around a corner and she staggers a little, almost falling into my lap.

The other passengers on the bus stare ahead blankly as I unhook an ear bud.

'Yes?'

She's smiling and nodding at me; I glance around. All the seats are occupied.

'Oh.'

Embarrassed, I scramble to pick up my bags, scarf, and umbrella. She slides into my seat, muttering something I can't quite catch. There's a dank, damp scent around her and I wonder for a moment where she's going, if she even has a home to go to.

The man I've been sitting next to maintains his resolute silence, shifting slightly, the better to stare out of the steamed-up window. I should say something, I think, but what? The bus lurches again, throwing me against the worn shopping trolley, and I grab at it to steady myself.

'Sorry.'

The man next to her rolls his eyes and mutters something under his breath, before swiping at the condensation on the window pane.

The old lady simply nods and smiles once more. She's wearing lipstick, a vivid red which is bleeding into the lines and wrinkles around her mouth. I smile back before turning to make my way carefully to the front of the bus. It's almost my stop, anyway.

The bus doors wheeze open and I step out onto the darkened street.

I don't know why I look back, but I do and there she is again. Struggling to get the shopping trolley down from the bus. She catches my eye, waves a hand helplessly.

'Here. Let me.'

She hovers behind me, encouragingly, unnervingly, as I pull at the trolley. I haul it onto the wet pavement as the bus drives away.

It's heavy and I feel the contents shift and clatter. There's a broken wheel, I notice as I let go of it, and a tear in the flap which forms the lid.

The old lady pats my hand as she thanks me. At least, I assume she's thanking me: she speaks a language I don't recognise, Russian perhaps, or Polish. Her hands are cold and I try not to flinch. I look down and see that she she's wearing heavy rings, two or three on each finger of each hand. And there's that smell again, as if something sweet is rotting.

I pull my hand away.

'You're welcome.'

I cross the road. Walk purposefully, I tell myself. Do not get sucked into ... into ...

Getting stuck with a charity case.

That's Daniel's voice. That's not helpful. Listening to Daniel. Do not look back.

I almost manage it, only turning as I reach the corner. But she's gone. The street is entirely empty, and somehow this comes as a relief.

As soon as I've locked the door behind me, I turn on the rest of the lights. I close the curtains, checking the window catches as I go.

I hang up my coat in the hallway, put the shopping in the kitchen, use the bathroom, find a towel and try to dry my hair. I kick off my boots. I don't like to wear shoes inside the flat: I'm too conscious that the people downstairs can hear me moving about as I can hear Katia, who lives in the attic flat above me.

On cue the floorboards above my head creak and I hear her shower running. She'll be off out later, Saturday night and all that. I take a moment to look around my flat: my books, my photographs.

Cold fingers gently brush my hand.

I wonder where she was going. The old lady.

She smiles.

Here I am. Safe.

I'm cooking a risotto when there's a knock at the door. It's Katia. I know it is. I've heard her leave her flat and clatter down the uncarpeted attic stairs. Carefully, I move the pan off the hob, before walking through into the hall.

She's there. In the living room.

This is not something I see. It's just a thought I have, quiet and distinct.

She's there.

I pause. The living room is empty. But there's a smell, something that wasn't there before. Something familiar. Katia thumps on the door again and I go to let her in.

'What took you so long? Never mind, don't tell me. What do you think?'

She steps back a little, grinning like an over-excited child. She's wearing an impossibly tiny mini-skirt and a thin, near-transparent shirt. Her shoes look cripplingly painful and she jangles and shines with cheap jewellery. Her thick auburn hair is gelled and spiked and she is wearing far too much make up. I resist the temptation to tell her to go back upstairs and fetch her coat.

'You look great. You know you do.'

'Well. It doesn't hurt to get a second opinion. So, are you coming out, or what?'

She does this every Saturday night. Dressed to kill, she calls in at my flat to invite me out with her.

It's almost funny.

'Well, you know ...'

I gesture towards the kitchen and Katia rolls her eyes. This is our little ritual. She asks me out. I say no. I'm older than her by a good ten years, yet it's always Katia who worries about me.

'Maybe next week,' I say.

She pulls me into a hug. She smells of lemon and honey and a heavy sweet perfume.

'You'll have to say yes sometime,' she whispers in my ear.

I go out all the time, I want to point out. To work. To shop. To the cinema. Then I feel her stiffen and step back. For a moment, she's looking beyond me, into the living room. She looks ... puzzled.

I turn and the room is empty. Of course it is. *She is not there.* Who is not there?

'So, I'll see you tomorrow, yeah?'

She's already halfway down the stairs.

I lock the door behind her and go back to the living room. Somehow the lights in here seem to have faded. The bookshelves are dusty, I notice. There's that sweet old-fashioned smell that I can't place hanging in the air. It's chilly too, as if no one has lived here for a long time. I turn up the heating and go back to the kitchen.

I wake up with a great gasp and for a moment I don't know where I am. I was dreaming about falling — blood in my hair and falling — I was dreaming about —

But it's gone. This happens to me quite a lot now. I forget things. That is, I am conscious that there is something I cannot remember; a word, a face, a place. I've been told that this is quite common after a head injury and that it will get better. Gradually, my memory will improve.

I push my fingers through my hair until I find the ridges of the scars. I was cold. That was it. There was someone next to me ... I flex my fingers, my hand is stiff. I could waste a day like this: sitting in bed, counting my heartbeat, worrying at my scars, fretting.

But I don't. I choose not to. I get up.

'God, you look awful.'

I used to drink in this pub all the time. It's pleasant enough. There's a lot of dark polished wood and huge mirrors on the walls and a couple of sofas squashed together near the open fire. It's the kind of place people can pass a long lunchtime in, which is why it's so busy on a Sunday, but somehow Katia can always find a way to occupy one of the sofas. She's sitting there now, nursing a large diet Coke and eating a sandwich.

'I'm a bit tired, that's all.'

I don't mention that I've been up since six, cleaning the flat, trying to get rid of the stale sweet scent that has somehow invaded it.

I sit down next to her, dropping a bundle of newspapers on the table. We do this every weekend: meet for lunch, read the papers, talk. She leans forward, inspecting my face.

'You haven't heard from Daniel, have you?'

I haven't heard from him in months. I don't think about him these days. I try not to.

'No. Course not. Nothing like that.'

She yawns and falls back onto the sofa.

'Well, I'm exhausted.'

'Did you have a good night?'

Katia grins.

'That would be telling.'

There's a mirror hanging over the fireplace just behind her, and as I glance up I feel a jolt of recognition as I see a small dark figure reflected there. I look behind me, but the room is crowded and she's nowhere to be seen. Katia kicks me gently on my leg.

'I said, that would be telling.'

'Right. Yeah. Look, do you want a drink?'

If I go to the bar, I can check the room properly, I can see if she's there. But Katia gets to her feet instead.

'No. It's my turn. Besides, I want to see if Alfie's in, catch up on the gossip.'

Alfie works here and like most men, he's utterly smitten with Katia. I wonder sometimes if they've ever been more than friends, but I don't quite dare ask. She pushes her way to the bar and I pick up a section of the newspaper. But instead of reading it I find myself gazing idly at Katia's receding reflection. There's a smear down one side of the mirror, so where I'm sitting is blurry, distorted. I lean forward so I can see myself more clearly, and the grey smudge seems to move too before resolving itself into a hazy figure, curving around me.

My vision blurs, my stomach churns, and I feel sick.

The old lady smiles and leans over me, reaching for my hand. Her face is wrinkled, grimy and grey. I do not want her to touch me — *No* — but then her hand is on mine, burning with cold. Her grip tightens as she repeats a single word again and again and now I understand.

Darling, my darling.

I pull my hand away and stand up abruptly, whirling around, knocking the table askew with my leg. But she's gone.

I'm standing up by the fireplace, pages of newsprint tumbling to the floor. She is not there. She is not there. It's too hot here, too crowded and I want to get away. At the bar, Alfie sees me, frowns and leans over the counter, saying something to Katia. She glances over and sighs before picking up her glass and my coffee and making her way back to the table.

'There you go.'

She sets the cup and glass down and sits, even though it's perfectly obvious she'd rather be flirting with Alfie. I sit down next to her, pick up my cup.

'Shall I tell you about my new man then?'

Katia has a never-ending succession of new men. She bounces from one relationship to another with maddening ease. Her heart, apparently, is quite impervious to shock or grief.

She kicks me again.

'Well?'

Sometimes I think it's all we ever talk about.

'Sure. I want to hear all about him.'

She wasn't there. She can't have been there.

Pushing her hair out of her eyes, Katia leans forward and it's only then that I realise she's still wearing the same clothes I saw her in yesterday evening.

'Haven't you been home yet?'

My voice is sharper than I'd intended, and all at once Katia's giddy good humour vanishes.

'You know what? I've had enough of this.'

She finishes her drink and stands.

'You are not my mother and I don't have to answer to you or anyone else. What I do with my life is my business — and at least I have a life.'

Some people have stopped talking and are staring at us, Katia snatches up her bag and is out of the door before I can even begin to apologise.

I hate arguments.

Alfie comes over to the table, picks up Katia's abandoned glass and plate, and then wipes up a few breadcrumbs. There is that smell again — damp, decaying, stronger now — and something else, a perfume, *Lily of the Valley*. She's sitting right next to me. But she's not, she can't be.

'You alright?'

Tears spring to my eyes.

'Yeah.'

'She's got a bit of a temper, Katia.'

He almost sounds approving and I dredge up an unconvincing smile.

'Yeah.'

Alfie wipes over the same section of table again. In the corner of my eye, a shadow moves and I feel her breath on my neck.

'Are you sure you're alright? You know ...'

He makes a vague gesture towards his forehead. Next to me, she whispers in my ear,

Friends keep secrets.

He knows, I realise, he knows: Katia must have told him. I stare at him for a moment or two, before he smiles sympathetically and goes back to the bar.

There's nothing left to do but go home.

I'm in the kitchen, on my hands and knees, scrubbing out a cupboard when I hear it. There's a soft thud which is followed by slow muffled footsteps. I dry my hands and get to my feet, reach over and turn off the radio. I listen. It's not upstairs. It's here, in the flat.

Katia. Katia's come down because she wants to apologise. I don't move, I stand and listen, waiting for her to call out. Only of course it isn't her, because she would have said something by now, and anyway, Katia would never just walk in. Even if the door wasn't locked, she wouldn't do that to me. There's that smell again, that stink of unwashed skin and sweet perfume.

My darling.

There's no one there. There can't be.

My darling.

In the living room, someone sighs. I hear them shuffling around the room, muttering under their breath.

I go in. The lamp, the lamp I always leave on in this room, flickers and dies. Automatically, I reach for the light switch by the door.

And then I see her.

She's by the window, looking out into the street. The closer I look, the clearer she becomes. Her hair is matted and greying. Her long black coat is threadbare in places, with pockets that sag and bulge, I can see that her shoes are actually mud-stained trainers and one arthritic hand, twisted and misshapen, rests gently on the window pane. I flex my fingers. Tap. Tap. Tap.

She's pleased to see me.

Darling.

I back out of the room into the hallway.

Why do you always do this?

I'm crying. I don't understand what I've done wrong.

Why?

He shoves me. Hard.

Darling.

Then he slaps me.

The woman stands at the window. This is her home now.

I back away. If I can get to the door — The second slap knocks me off my feet and as I fall my head hits the wrought iron radiator. My scalp splits to the bone.

Bitch.

I'm crawling now, desperately trying to brace myself for the kick I know is coming — but I'm blinded by blood and still I feel that I'm falling, that the floor is tilting away from me. Part of me wants to give in, to slip away into the darkness where he can't reach me.

There's a banging at the door. There's a voice.

I can feel her getting closer as I scramble on my hands and knees into the hall.

I pull myself to my feet, but fingers can't manage the bolt and lock. I can't see, there's something in my eyes. I can feel her breath on my neck, and my skin prickles as she reaches out to stroke my hair.

But when I wheel around to push her away, there's no one there. No one. I let my legs give way, and slowly I slide to the floor again, the door at my back, struggling to catch my breath. The hallway is empty.

Who can I tell?

No one.

When you've been hospitalised due to a massive head trauma, people don't really listen to you any more, or so I've found. They prefer to diagnose you. Headaches? Mood swings? Depression, anxiety, panic attacks? Take a pill, see a therapist, pull yourself together. There's no telling anyone, I understand that straight away, because somehow during the past year, I have stopped being a person and become a collection of symptoms.

What does she want?

My darling.

Me. She wants me.

No. No. No. I will not lose it. I will not lose control. I close my eyes. Her voice fades away a little and I'm able to breathe more steadily. I am here in my own home. I am safe. A bubble of hysteria rises and I can't catch my breath.

A hand stretches out to stroke my hair.

I will not lose control.

Relax your fingers, one by one. Breathe in for the count of three, hold for three then exhale for three. Repeat. Repeat. Repeat.

I'm aware that the woman is there, hovering anxiously over me, but I don't look, I won't look. Gradually I realise that if I don't make eye contact, then she can't quite reach me. I don't know how long I sit there, shaking, my head in my hands, before I'm able to stand and open the door.

Katia won't answer, although I'm sure she's inside her flat. Eventually, I go back downstairs. Instead of using my key, I sit on the bare wooden stairs and lean my head against the banister. I close my eyes. Katia is my only friend, and now she won't talk to me.

Friends keep secrets.

I won't listen. I won't.

I hear a door open. I hear the stairs creak. I smell her perfume. I'm afraid to open my eyes.

Friends keep secrets.

'Hey.'

Katia.

'Move up then.'

She sits down next to me. I want to explain, but I don't know what to say, I don't know how to say it. No one will believe me anyway.

'I'm sorry. I've got a rotten hangover.'

I nod.

'You're not getting those headaches again, are you?'

'No. Nothing like that.'

Headaches, dreadful blinding headaches, were one of the side effects, at first. I realise that I'm scratching my scalp again; tracing over the starburst scars that no one can see. That no one knows about, except Katia. And Daniel.

Gently, Katia takes my hand in hers.

'God, you're freezing.'

I'll never be warm again.

'Do you want to see a doctor? I'll go with you.'

And say what? I saw an old lady and she held my hand? And now I can't get rid of her, she's here in the surgery, Doctor, just there in the corner of my eye. Can't you see her? No, of course you can't, she is my own, my own private —

I shake my head.

'I'm fine. Really. I'm sorry. I just wanted to apologise for being such a … mess.'

'Don't be daft.'

'Katia?'

I don't want to ask. I don't want to hear the answer.

'Have you ever told anyone about, you know, about Daniel? About what he did?'

Katia smiles at me reassuringly, her knee nudging mine, then she lets go of my hand.

'I promised I wouldn't, didn't I?'

Liar.

'Do you want to come up to mine? We can have a cup of tea and a catch-up.'

All I can think about is the look on Alfie's face. He knows. I feel sick and ashamed all over again. Who else has she told?

'Another time, yeah? I've got stuff to do.'

I stand up.

I busy myself with my keys until I'm sure Katia's back inside her flat. She is there in the corner of my eye, as she has been all along. The best I can manage is not to look, to push her to one side somehow. I open the door and breathe in slowly. We go in.

I'm awake long before the alarm rings on Monday morning. To tell the truth, I haven't slept at all. I've spent most of the night trying to work things out. Trying to understand.

She won't leave: I know that for certain, just as I'm sure that I can't reason with her. Just as I know that for as long as she clings to me there will be no joy in my life, no light or warmth. All it took was a little kindness to let her in.

No good deed goes unpunished.

Daniel used to say that all the time. I've been thinking about that a lot. All night, really.

I wish I could say that I have the courage to go to Daniel's office on my own, but I know I don't. I take my time dressing, choosing sober, sensible, respectable clothes. My long black winter coat, hat, scarf, gloves. I do not look in the mirror. I ignore the urge to turn and face her, or worse, speak to her: I simply let her follow. Then I go up to Katia's flat.

I know she doesn't work on Mondays so I knock and wait.

'Jesus. Who died?'

I've obviously woken her: she leans against the door jamb looking both befuddled and resentful.

There's nothing to do other than blurt it out.

'I need to see Daniel. Will you come with me?'

I can't do this if Katia doesn't come with me. But I don't know how to persuade her. She gives me that look. That *when will she pull herself together* look.

Please, Katia. Please.

'Fine. Fine. Come in while I get dressed. Come on.'

Daniel still works as a solicitor in the same firm in the city centre. The company offices are in a smart Georgian townhouse. Imposing. Immaculate.

'Tell me again why we're here?'

It's a bitterly cold day and Katia's jacket is too short and too thin. We've been here for an hour or so and her patience is running out.

'I just want to see him. Talk to him.'

She snorts.

'I tell you what. Let me talk to him. I've got a couple of things I'd like to say.'

Daniel never liked Katia, I remember. He disapproved of her. *Friends keep secrets.*

I blink. Shift a little. If I don't look, if I ignore her for just a little while longer. This isn't much of a plan, I know. But it's all I've got. I don't deserve this, I don't deserve her. He does.

'Can we go and get a coffee?'

Before I can answer, Daniel walks out of the front door. He walks purposefully down the steps, like the busy man he is. He looks well. Successful. Decent.

'Well?'

Katia nudges me.

'There he is.'

The last time I saw Daniel, we were quarrelling. The last time I heard his voice, he was so angry with me, enraged. My head aches. By the time I came home from hospital, he was gone. I hear his voice. There's that bright blossom of pain. I can't move.

'Jesus! He's getting away!'

Katia has grabbed my hand and is dragging me across the road.

'Oi! Dickhead!'

The street is busy and Daniel doesn't hear. Doesn't seem to hear. *Darling. My darling.*

I can't bear this anymore.

By now, Daniel has got as far as the taxi rank at the corner of the street.

'Daniel!'

He stops and turns around. He sees us, running towards him. Do I imagine it? That flicker of distaste as he recognises us. Me.

Not my problem.

His taxi pulls away just as we get to the corner.

'Shit!'

Katia is furious, trembling with rage.

'He saw us, you know. Shit! Shit!'

Not my problem.

What was I thinking? Even if he had stopped, Daniel wouldn't have seen her, that's not how it works. It takes a little kindness, to let her in and once she is there, she will never let go. Just a little kindness, and Daniel has none.

Suddenly, I too feel the cold, cutting right through my coat. The effort of not looking at her, of ignoring that persistent nudge, is wearing me away. I give in. I turn and look and I see that she's standing just in front of Daniel's building. The more I focus the more solid she becomes. There she is, in full daylight.

She's standing close to the edge of the pavement, shopping trolley to hand. Too close, I realise. The trolley tilts and falls, scattering tins and jars into the oncoming traffic. She turns, takes a shuffling half step, then another. None of the cars slow, no passer-by gives her a glance.

'Jesus. Isn't anyone going to help her?'

Katia can see.

Daniel despised Katia and her compassion, but I have come to rely on it. Of course she can see her. She sets off to help before I can stop her.

Katia was never afraid of Daniel: she hammered and screamed at the door until he let her in that night. She called an ambulance, she stayed with me. No-one else cared. No-one else dared interfere.

And now, still furious at Daniel, more than anything else, she strides up the street to help again. I could call out, stop her. But I don't.

I watch her haul the shopping trolley out of the road, then pick up the tins and jars and bottles out of the gutter as cars continue to speed by.

Friends keep secrets.

The old lady flutters helplessly to one side, gesturing as she speaks, the rings on her fingers gleaming dully as she circles the trolley.

Darling. My darling.

She reaches forward to take Katia's hand and instead of shouting out a warning, I hold my breath and wait for the weak winter sunlight to warm my skin once more.

Richard Smyth contributed the title story to our anthology
Crying Just Like Anybody, *and makes a welcome*
return to our pages with this Yorkshire story.

Chalklands

Richard Smyth

It's nearly Guy Fawkes Night. I'm told the weather is going to be clear this year, a nice night for a bonfire. But I will stay home, all the same.

My father, who was a history teacher at the All Saints School, told me what they did to Guy Fawkes, after they caught him. They chopped him into pieces — they chopped him into four pieces, my father said, easy as slicing up a quiche. They chopped him up and left his insides lying in the dirt of the Old Palace Yard.

My father said that they then delivered the four pieces of Guy Fawkes to the four corners of the kingdom. I asked my father what happened to them when they got there. My father said that in Cornwall they put his left foot in a pasty. In Ireland they mixed up stout and potatoes and made a stew of his right hand. His left hand went to Scotland, where they sewed it up in a prize-winning haggis, and his right foot was skinned, fried and served up with chips and vinegar on the seafront at Scarborough.

But it was Guy Fawkes's insides that bothered me. They just left them there. There would have been rats, rooks, crows, all fighting over his insides — while they were still warm, I expect. Kites, too. They had red kites in London in those days.

They almost went extinct, red kites. We almost wiped them out, but now apparently we're bringing them back. My brother, David, is very into all that sort of thing. A few years ago, he and his wildlife society helped with the reintroduction programme; they released twelve red kites into the wild at Holderness. David got an MBE for it.

I see them now, sometimes, when I'm out walking on the Wolds: indolent, elegant, winnowing their forked tail feathers in the wind. I see them, and I think of Guy Fawkes's guts.

I wish they had gone extinct. I wish we had wiped them out.

In any case, I like it up there, on the Wolds. Chalklands have a sort of gentleness to them. I feel that, even now, even after what happened. There are barrows up there, burial mounds, dozens of them: Garrowby, Rudston, Bal Hill, Maiden's Grave. I've always thought that it must be a nice place to be buried.

We argued over that, my father, David, and I, when Theresa died.

'We can't just burn her,' I said. 'That's what you do with witches.'

'It's called *cremation*,' David said. He was thirteen then. 'It's not burning. There's flowers and you sing hymns and everything, and the Father still says a Mass. They wouldn't do that for a witch, would they? And anyway there aren't any witches, there isn't even such a thing.'

'There's flowers on the Wolds,' I muttered. It was true, there were, and there still are, whole meadows of them, if you know where to look: harebells, poppies, wild mignonette. And you can sing hymns there, if you want to. (I do, sometimes.)

My father was quiet, at first. He was a Catholic, of course, a Corkman's son raised in south Liverpool, and had a Catholic's qualms about the practice of cremation. But then, too, there was a Celtic pagan streak in him as wide as the River Lee.

I think my mother, my mad mother from the Yorkshire chalklands, brought that out in him — and when Theresa died, he found himself thinking of my mother.

'It'll be a cremation,' he said, at last, interrupting our bickering. 'Father Gillen will say the Mass. You, Mary, will gather the flowers, from wherever you please. It'll be beautiful, I promise you.'

I had to bite my lip to keep from crying. I looked at my father and thought I could see flames dancing in his dark eyes. I wondered if in those flames he saw my mother's flame-red hair.

I don't remember my mother. Theresa did. I asked her once what she was like, when the two of us were out walking in the hills above Wintringham.

'She was a crackpot,' Theresa said. 'She was always singing. Even when she was angry. Especially when she was angry. The angrier she was, the louder she sang.' Theresa kicked at a clump of dandelions. For a minute I thought she was going to cry. 'She cooked horrible food. Liver and tripe and black pudding. And she dressed like a mad woman and never combed her hair. When she took me to school, everyone laughed at her.'

'What did she do?'

'She just laughed back.'

We walked for miles that day. We walked east, into the sunrise. We walked so far that when I breathed in I thought I could smell salt and seaweed. I was ten; Theresa was fifteen.

I'm not ten any more, but Theresa will always be fifteen.

It happened about three weeks after that day, that walk. It wasn't just me and Theresa: David was with us too. It was October, half-term. We were going to walk to Bishop Wilton, eat the sandwiches our father had made for us, and walk back. It would have taken us all day.

But we never made it to Bishop Wilton. We never made it further than Greet's Hill — we never made it further than the place there where a rough chalk cliff juts from the meadowland, and the off-white rocks tumble down a hundred feet to the valley floor.

Theresa walked in front as we climbed through the meadows. The precipice of Greet's Hill made a ragged triangle against the sky up ahead. David, throwing a cricket ball from hand to hand, walked behind her. I was the youngest, the smallest, and I walked at the back.

I remember David stopping, and pointing upwards, and I think he laughed and shouted something; but he was too far ahead for me to hear. He was pointing at a bird, a big bird overhead. It must have been a buzzard, or a raven, because this was thirty-five years ago, and there were no kites in the chalklands then — so it must have been a trick of the new-risen sun, but I thought I saw flame-red feathers flash as the bird yawed into the wind.

Three hours later our father found us sobbing by the side of the A road. That is, he found me and David. He had driven behind the wailing ambulance and now, with us stumbling and weeping at his heels, he chased the ambulancemen across the chalklands, across the four miles to the foot of the Greet's Hill cliff.

It took perhaps an hour. We were too late, we were all too late. We knew we would be, David and me. We knew nothing could be done. We'd seen Theresa fall — we'd peered, terrified, over the edge, and seen her body splayed motionless in a chalkstone ghyll.

Afterwards I tried to talk to my father.

'We couldn't stop her, Dad. I shouted as loud as I could.'

'I know, darling. Hush, now. I know. You're tired. It's not the time for talking. Hush now. We can talk later, and you can tell me — you can tell me all about it.' He smiled, distractedly, and stroked the back of my neck. 'Sleep now, my darling,' he said.

When the lights were out, I slipped from beneath my blankets and crept over to David's bed. David was facing away from me, pretending to sleep. I knelt beside his bed, placed a hand on his shoulder, and whispered in his ear: 'Did you see her?'

I felt his body stiffen.

'See who?'

'You know who.'

'I don't, I *don't*,' he hissed, and clutched his pillow about his head. I went back to bed. I didn't sleep.

It wasn't till afterwards, after the funeral — after we'd *committed her to the flames* — after I'd stood in the sunlit churchyard and watched the smoke that was once my sister's body drift and diffuse in the ice-blue sky; it wasn't till then that I went again to my father, and told him what happened on the chalklands at Greet's Hill, and it wasn't until then that my father told me why.

We were in the kitchen. Just the two of us. My father had poured himself a glass of whisky. He sat at the table in his black suit with the whisky at his elbow and just stared at nothing.

When I started talking, it was as though he wasn't listening — as though he couldn't even hear me, even though I was right there, right at his side, with one hand clutching, while I spoke, at the rough serge of his jacket sleeve. But when I had finished, he nodded, and took a mouthful of whisky, and without looking at me said quietly: 'I knew, of course. I knew.'

Then he gathered me up with one arm around my waist and pulled me on to his lap. He kissed my hair.

'You were a baby,' he murmured. I could smell the whisky and the mild, medicinal perfume of the oil he wore on his hair. 'David was nearly two. You were both with me, in the study. I was reading.' He paused, swallowed, and exhaled a long, tremulous breath. 'Your mother was downstairs. Theresa was with her. They were doing something in the kitchen, I don't know what.' Again a pause. I could feel him shivering. 'It was the fire,' he said. 'The fire in the living room. She always built it up too high, your mother did. It wasn't safe, the logs piled up like that. But she liked a big fire in the fireplace. She used to make paper dollies out of newspaper — she took sheets of newspaper, from the *Observer*, and twisted them up into dollies. Then she'd set them in the fireplace, in among the kindling, and then she'd light them, to get the fire going. I can still picture her face, when she was making the dollies. She'd be so intent. And there'd be ink on her skin — from her fingers, from the newsprint.' He kissed my hair. 'She was beautiful, your mother,' he said.

A log had rolled loose from the fireplace, he told me. It had set the hearthrug going, and then the carpet. Then the curtains.

With his cheek pressed to my hair, my father said: 'I carried you out of the study window. When smoke started coming under the door, and I heard the noise from downstairs. I took you and David in my arms and I climbed out on to the roof of the porch. Then I said a prayer, and jumped. I laid you both on the grass and covered you with my coat. And I went back inside.

'An old place like that, it doesn't take much for a fire to get out of control. All that timber. I ran down the hallway. I saw

Theresa's hand, her arm, waving in the smoke. I grabbed her, I picked her up. I shouted your mother's name. God, Mary, the heat! I couldn't stand it. No one could have stood it. No one could have.

'And Theresa in my arms was screaming, yelling. I ran, I ran out of the house. And d'you know what I wonder?' Again he sighed and I could smell the whisky on his breath. 'I wonder if she was screaming because she was frightened, because of the fire — or if she was screaming because she wanted to stay with her mother.'

'But she would have been burned!'

My father shrugged.

'I know. But still. In a way I felt that all I was doing was taking the poor child away from her mother. And I know that's stupid. For God's sake, I was saving my child's life!' He shook his head. 'But in a way I still feel that.'

I didn't understand. I was only ten years old. But of course my father didn't mean me to understand: he wasn't talking to me, wasn't talking to his daughter Mary. He was just talking.

Anyway, he was silent then for a while. He took another drink. I sat in his lap and listened to his breathing.

I had to ask. I didn't want to know the answer but I had to ask.

I put my head against his chest and asked: 'Did you see her? Did you see my mother?'

He rested his chin on the top of my head.

'Yes,' he said. 'I saw her. At the end of the passageway. There was too much fire, too much smoke. I couldn't get to her. She looked like she was waving. No. She looked like she was *dancing*.'

David, my brother, doesn't remember the fire. I asked him once. He said he knew there'd been a fire, that our mother had died in it. But he didn't remember it and he certainly didn't want to talk about it.

I expect David'll go on like that for the rest of his life, not talking about it, not talking about anything except his bloody red kites and his bloody MBE —

But that's not fair. I mean, I don't talk about it either. I didn't even talk to my father about it after that afternoon in the kitchen, even though he understood it all better than anyone. He understood why my mother came back. Why she took Theresa.

I suppose Theresa remembered it all. I suppose she loved our mother, even if she was a crackpot. Or whatever she was. That was why she ran to her, when she saw her — when we all saw her, on the cliff that day. That was why she ran to her, too fast, even though we screamed at her to stop, even when it wasn't safe, and she stumbled, and fell ...

That was why Theresa ran when she saw our flame-haired mother waving, or dancing, on the cliff edge.

It's easier to talk about it now that my father's gone. He died last week — quietly, peacefully. We buried him in a churchyard on the chalklands; there was a Father there to say the Mass, and there were flowers. In the sky overhead a burnished red kite soared and shrieked.

I threw stones at it. David tried to stop me, and the Father did too, but I stood in the churchyard and threw stones at it, and called it a damned bloody vulture, until it banked lazily to the west, and flapped beyond the hilltops, and left the chalklands behind.

Sometimes the most touching stories are also the simplest, as in this tale from Ann Wahlman.

Old Ghosts

Ann Wahlman

These days I retire well before everyone else I know. After darkness falls, I wait until the edges of sleep surround me before I start up the stairs to the bedroom. My husband and I have the best talks like this, when I am a bit sleepy, when we lie with limbs interwoven in bed. I love the feel of him next to me: his warm breath on my earlobe, the weight of his arm thrown over me, the way our bodies twist together in a complicated knot of comfort. These are the moments that I wouldn't trade for the world.

The book on my nightstand has gone neglected while my husband and I partake in our nightly talks. A thin layer of dust covers the pebbled fake leather binding: *The Works of Edgar Allan Poe*. It was what I was reading before all of this began. I was searching for old ghosts in ghost stories and gothic romances.

I switch off the light and pull the covers up to my chin, like I've done since I was a child. I wait with my eyes closed, breathing deeply, focusing my ears on the smallest sounds that creak through this old house. When I finally hear his footsteps, I can't help but smile. I know he won't talk to me until he's actually beside me in bed, until his lips are pressed up against my ear and he can say what he wants to without fear. It's an enchanted place, a protected space — this bed.

When I feel him settle in beside me, his arm go around my waist and his leg slip over mine, I can finally relax.

'Susan,' he softly sings into my ear. 'I love you.'

I talk about what I did at work that day. It's not an incredibly impressive list of things. I spend the early part of my days thinking about the previous night, and the latter part thinking about the coming one. My boss is worried that I'm withdrawn.

'He gave me the number of a psychiatrist his wife's sister sees,' I tell him.

I expect my husband to be indignant, but he's not. After a few moments, he says, 'Maybe you *should* see someone.'

'I'm doing fine,' I say. 'I even went out to lunch with Karen today.'

He asks me how it went and I tell him it was fine. I don't mention that I broke down sobbing in the middle of the restaurant, that I had to hide in the bathroom for twenty minutes until the ache in my chest had passed.

I tell him how much I miss him.

'But you saw me last night,' he whispers.

'That's not the point,' I say. 'I never see you during the day.'

He is quiet, but I know he is still there. Even with my eyes closed, I can feel the heat from his breath on my neck.

'It's our anniversary tomorrow,' I say suddenly, as if this thought had somehow escaped me — it hasn't. 'It's our bronze anniversary.'

'Are we going out to celebrate?' he asks, and it hurts me that he can't remember. It's as if the night has erased his memory, wiped the slate clean.

He might not remember any of it, but I do. It's funny how your life can change in an entire instant, how you can spend the rest of your life chasing after old ghosts, trying to hold on to something that has simply vanished, something that has disappeared right in front of you into thin air.

'Are you crying?' he asks, when I wipe a tear from my still closed eye.

'I miss you,' I say again.

We fall asleep like that, caught between sorrow and love and memory. When the sun wakes me in the morning, he is gone. The covers on his side of the bed are smooth and straight, as if he'd never been there at all. Mornings are always like this for me, the acknowledgement of his disappearance and the acceptance of the day ahead; the long day that stretches endlessly without him the closer we are to summer.

I dream of moving to Alaska someday. There's a little town at the northernmost tip called Barrow that has twenty-four hours of night from the third week in November until the third week in January, but there are another two months where the sun never sets. The waiting would drive me insane.

The next day, when my mother calls me at a quarter past ten, I rush through the office to the handicapped bathroom where I can lock the door and talk in private.

'How are you doing?' she asks.

'Fine,' I tell her.

'Are you at work?'

'Of course I'm at work,' I say.

She spends the next five minutes telling me that I should have taken a personal day and the five after that telling me it's time to move on.

'I know they say it's totally normal to feel this way, Susie, but it's been nearly two years.' When I don't reply, she says, 'Don't you think enough is enough?'

I put a paper toilet seat cover on the white plastic seat and sit down on it.

'I want you to come over tomorrow night,' she says. 'I'm having a little dinner party for a few people at church, and it would be good for you to get out.'

'Mom,' I say, 'I'm not ready.'

'Seven o'clock sharp,' she says, as if I hadn't even spoken.

When I tell my husband about it that night, enveloped in his embrace, he tells me I should go. 'She's right, it will be good for you,' he says. 'You can't stay cooped up here like this forever.'

I tell him that I'd like nothing better than to stay in this bed with him until the sun burns out.

'That won't happen for another six billion years, honey,' he says. 'I think by then you'll be dead.'

'Don't talk like that,' I tell him.

'Everybody dies,' he says.

Plenty of people have died that I know. I think death is easier on people who believe, people like my mother who know in their hearts they will meet again when they cross over to the other side. I'm an atheist; maybe that's my problem. Maybe that's why I can't get over this, why I can't bounce back and other people can. I know that now is all I have, that there's nothing else out there when I die, that I'll never see my husband ever again. Maybe that's why I cling so fiercely to this old ghost that haunts me.

'You're not really here,' I tell my husband.

'What do you mean?' he asks. 'I'm right here.'

I feel his chin on my shoulder and his arm draped across my belly, it all points to his existence, to his presence. 'If I open my eyes,' I say, 'you'll disappear.'

'How do you know that?' he asks.

'You're always gone in the morning,' I tell him.

'Maybe I'm just an early riser,' he says.

'No,' I say, 'you're a figment of my imagination.'

He's quiet for a while, and I can hear the sound of his steady breathing. Finally he says, 'How do you know?'

I press my lips together in the dark. I tell him it's what the last shrink told me, right before she prescribed me some kind of an antipsychotic — a prescription which I never filled.

'Why didn't you take it?' he asks.

'I was afraid you'd disappear,' I say.

He tells me he'll stay as long as I want him to, as long as I need him to. It comforts me to think that in a half-dozen billion years when the sun winks out, when there is nothing left but darkness, we'll still be having our nightly talks.

My mother's dinner party consists of some hors d'oeuvres, French onion dip, whisky sours, and a pasta bake. White-haired ladies from her church sit with paper plates of appetisers poised on their skirted laps, while the men sip straight whisky. There's a young couple my age sporting new wedding bands and a tall, slim guy named Robert with no date. The blatant inclusion of one coupled pair my age to offset the single guy makes it obvious this is a set-up.

'Damn it, Mom,' I stage whisper to her in the kitchen while refilling an hors d'oeuvre plate, 'I told you I wasn't ready.'

'Robert's a nice boy, Susie,' she says. 'Just give him a chance.'

The ease of Robert's blush tells me that he wasn't in on the plan for tonight. Neither of us mentions it aloud, but our tight, awkward smiles to each other say we both know my mother's intention.

'So what do you do?' I venture as the party gets into full swing around us.

He tells me he's an accountant of some kind, goes on about it for a good two minutes, although I'm not really listening.

I murmur, 'Oh, that's nice.'

When he returns the question, I have to force the gears in my head to turn to formulate an answer. Somehow my brain can't come up with the words I've spit out at every other party I've ever gone to.

Midway through the party and after a few whisky sours, Robert loosens up. He starts smiling a little more, standing a little closer, even touching my arm a few times. It occurs to me that I could see myself with someone like Robert: someone smart and a little awkward with a decent sense of humour, someone who is happy with the small things, contented with life as it is. I wonder what my husband will think of this, whether the queen-size bed is big enough for the three of us.

'You know,' I say. 'I think I left the iron on. I've got to go.'

As I slip out the door, I hear him ask, 'Don't those things turn themselves off these days?'

When I get home, I undress hurriedly, throwing clothes around the room. Before all of this, I'd never have done that. I'd have put everything away: my husband's socks, newspapers, shoes, books, and discarded clothing. But I'm not the same person I was then, either.

'You didn't stay all that late,' my husband says as his arm threads itself around me. He kisses my neck. 'Did you have a good time?'

I tell him yes first, then no, and finally say maybe. When he asks what happened, I admit to him that my mother set me up.

He laughs. 'How'd that go?' he asks.

'Not well,' I admit. 'I lied about the iron being on and left.'

'Well, at least you went,' he says.

'I don't know about this Robert guy,' I say.

He tells me I should see how it goes, that he sounds like a nice guy. He says I deserve to be happy.

'What will happen to you?' I ask him.

'I told you I'd stay as long as you needed me,' my husband says.

I ask him if he'll just disappear one day.

'I already have,' he tells me.

My husband keeps his promise in the following weeks. There are a number of dinners with Robert, a few movies, a dozen or so walks. Robert has even been inside the house, downstairs on the couch while we sipped wine and watched television. I've cooked for him a couple of times, but he always leaves whenever bedtime approaches. I've never had to ask him to go. I don't know if it's because of the religious thing or if he intuitively knows I have my own routine when it comes to my sleeping arrangements. Maybe he won't want to have sex until after we're married.

After I kiss Robert goodnight and close the door behind him, I hurry upstairs and undress, pull back the covers and turn out the light. Every night I'm afraid my husband won't show up, but each time he slides into bed next to me and throws his leg over mine.

'How'd it go?' he asks.

'Do you really want to know?' I ask him.

'Of course,' he replies. 'I want to know that you're happy.'

'I wouldn't go that far,' I say.

He tells me not to string Robert along too long. He worries that I might sabotage the relationship and run away to Alaska like I've threatened. I tell him I'll get a summer house in Antarctica where we can be together.

'It's winter there then,' I say. 'I could get a research position studying the effects of darkness on humans and animals.'

'Don't you dare,' he says. 'Your life is here.'

I want to argue with him that I don't have a life, but I can't. It snuck up on me in the daylight while I wasn't looking.

'You come to bed later and later these days,' he says. His voice is heavy and sad.

He's right: I spend so much time with Robert that my husband and I barely have much time before I fall asleep. Some nights we hardly talk at all; others I'm so wired I can't seem to close my eyes so that he can visit me.

'I'm sorry,' I say.

He takes a deep breath and lets out a contented sigh. 'I'm not,' he whispers into my ear.

One night a little while later, Robert doesn't go home directly after dinner. We sit on the couch and finish our wine, and I make coffee.

I watch him from the doorway in the kitchen as the coffee maker gurgles. I see how comfortably he sits on the couch I bought with my husband, the one we argued over because he thought pink floral wasn't manly enough. Robert doesn't seem to mind the décor; he seems perfectly at ease, sitting back in the cushions with one leg crossed over the other. He laughs at something on the television and takes a sip from his wine glass, which is almost empty.

When he looks up and sees me watching him, he asks, 'What?'

'Nothing,' I say.

He looks from me to the television and back again, and then smiles. I sit next to him on the couch, let him put his arm around me and pull me close.

We kiss on the couch like teenagers and forget about the coffee. When the time comes for Robert to go, he simply doesn't. I don't ask him to stay and I never mention leaving. We only walk up the stairs together to the bedroom. At the doorway, I pause with my hand on the light switch. The bed is perfectly made, the comforter smoothed flat, the pillows fluffed and perched at the proper angle. A pile of books rests on the nightstand, all unread.

'Is something wrong?' Robert asks. His hand is on my shoulder, his chin pressed against the top of my head.

'No,' I say. Although I expect to find something out of place, some sign that some old ghost has been here, everything is just as I left it.

I lead Robert to the bed where we undress each other and slip under the covers together. I don't bother to turn out the light and he doesn't request it. We make love under the unflattering artificial brightness; the whole time, I keep my eyes open.

'Listen to them — the children of the night. What music they make!' Dracula was referring to the wolves outside his castle, but he might as well have been talking about the two violinists in Linda Brucesmith's story.

The 25th Caprice

Linda Brucesmith

The Carnegie Hall audience rarely rises to its feet before a performance. 'Yes, yes,' thinks Pesha. The orchestra is also standing. The strings tap their bows against their music stands.

It is the fiftieth anniversary of Pesha's concert debut; images of his eight-year-old self have been resurrected everywhere. Throughout the celebrations he has been troubled by headaches and a hunted sensation. He has not slept well. Moodily, he lifts his Guarnerius, settles it beneath his chin. He anticipates the cutting of the lights. He will use the black to gather himself: the performance will not commence until the silence is absolute.

But even the dark is restless.

In the front row, there is whispering. Someone says, 'Shh.'

Then something hits him in the chest — a small thing, which falls at his feet.

When the first spotlight picks him out, Pesha looks at the floor. He sees a red apple core, neatly nibbled. Its presence — and that of its dispatcher in the front stalls — fills him with melancholy. Transfixed, he picks up the core, calls for a stool, positions it on the seat. He steps back, into the dark; the spotlight follows him. 'No,' he says, looking into the light and pointing. 'There!' The light wavers a little, tracks back to the stool. The image of the neatly nibbled core appears on the screens behind the orchestra.

Pesha fingers the tune to a nursery rhyme; he serenades the apple core. He follows with another brilliantly rendered rhyme, then another. The orchestra shuffles sheet music, downs instruments, and sits. There is no interval and no champagne. The apple core stays where it is.

After every piece Pesha bows to a stunned house, to the apple marksman's now empty seat, then to the core. Eventually, he undoes his tie. Grasping his bow in one hand and his violin in the other, he holds them above his head. On the screens behind, his magnified face is as pale as moonlight.

Shots of applause run through the house.

Then a man in the third row tosses his programme into the air. He stands, edges past the knees of those still seated. Others do the same. Uncertain whether they should feel embarrassed, cheated, or insulted, they get to their feet and leave.

Pesha turns to the orchestra, makes a contrite face for the bewildered conductor. He transfers his bow to his violin hand, blows a kiss to the core and departs the stage. Preoccupied by a thunderous ache in his temples he hurries down corridors, past walls hung with cables, past stage hands and technicians who dip their heads then stare at his retreating back. When he reaches his dressing room he steps inside, closes the door and leans against it. Soothed by the dark, he draws the curtains and opens a window. The lights of the city fill the room with a cool illumination.

A tall, thin man is sitting in his armchair. He is wearing black trousers and a tailcoat, a white linen shirt, cravat, and a high-collared waistcoat. His forearms run longer than the chair's armrests; his knees extend past the cushions supporting his thighs.

'An astonishing performance, Pesha!' The thin man's voice is full of highs and lows; his hands leap into the air like birds. 'Please, sit down.' Fingers fluttering, he directs Pesha to a chair. He removes a red apple from the fruit bowl on Pesha's coffee table and nibbles neatly.

An astonishing performance? Pesha is bothered by the sense he has just now returned from somewhere, but is unable to recall quite where.

'Let's get down to business,' the thin man says. 'Tonight was my little joke — though I *could* unmake you. Like that,' he aims, throws his part-eaten apple out through the window, 'I could do it. But that would mean finding someone else and, God knows, finding you took long enough. It is time, Pesha. We are due.'

There is a loud knock on the dressing room door. Pesha hurries to open it. In the time it takes his manager, Max, to stride into the room — his publicist, Suzanne, hurrying after him — he glimpses a gaggle of wide-eyed faces in the corridor outside. Suzanne waves them away. She closes the door while Max switches on the light. Her face is white with concern. His is red and outraged.

'What are you doing in the dark?' Max blusters. Grasping Pesha's elbow, he moves him towards the armchair; the thin man has disappeared. Pesha shrugs Max off, steps to the window, looks out at the city and searches the street below. Turning, he avoids the armchair and sinks into the couch beside Max. Suzanne remains standing. In Max's presence she will not sit beside Pesha or press her hand to his cheek.

'What was that out there tonight?' Max says. 'There's a conductor swearing to boycott everything we do! An audience that doesn't know whether to laugh or cry! I don't know whether to laugh or cry! Which is it? Should I laugh or cry?'

Pesha is still. Shock contorts his face. There, in his mind's eye, the entire performance is replayed. He clears his throat, looks from Max to Suzanne. Her fingers are pressed to her lips; in Max's presence, he will not console her. 'Max, my friend. I think we cry.'

Press clips are spread across Max's desk. The New York concert is big news. The Times has prepared a mock interview with the apple core. Someone has sent a T-shirt: on the front is a red violin with a bite taken out.

'I don't care! Find Pesha and get him here,' Max shouts into the phone. He slams it down. Immediately, it rings. Max grabs the receiver, 'Schönberg here ... no, Marty, we've said all we're going to say, you'll have to rethink your deadlines like everyone else.' He hangs up again.

There is a tap on his office door.

'For God's sake. What?'

Suzanne grimaces, pushes her curls back from her forehead, opens the door. She is carrying a basket of red apples tied with a red satin ribbon. 'They're from the people at the Sydney Opera House. You've got to return their calls, Max.'

Max snorts. 'Everyone's a comedian. Get rid of the apples, Suzanne. Eat them, make sauce, I don't care. Just goddamn find Pesha.'

Two days later, the Australians call direct. 'We don't like what we're hearing, Max.'

'It's nothing,' says Max.

'Can you give us Pesha, in Sydney, in two weeks?'

'I can.'

'We've got full houses. There'll be hell to pay if you don't.'

Every day at noon, Pesha waits for Suzanne in front of her building. As the autumn sun shines on its white marble, he tucks himself into a corner until she emerges. Together they hurry down Fifth Avenue, past the Pulitzer Fountain, into Central Park. They sit on a bench overlooking the pond, eat lunch.

Two weeks after the apple core incident, Pesha waits while Suzanne unwraps her sandwich. He bites into his bread roll and gazes across the water to the arched stonework of Gapstow Bridge.

He sighs, then says, 'How much do you know about Niccolò Paganini?'

'The devil's fiddler? As much as anyone, I suppose.'

'He liked the dark, preferred to play on stage by candlelight, did you know that?'

'Like you.' She is pleased by the comparison.

'Nothing like me. Completely different,' Pesha mutters.

Carefully, Suzanne says, 'Tell me about Paganini.'

'After he died, people said they heard him play from his coffin. Do you think that's possible?' He watches her closely.

'Do I believe dead bodies in wooden boxes play violins?' Suzanne can't help herself. 'No. There wouldn't be enough elbow room.'

Pesha ignores her. 'He died at fifty-eight, of throat cancer.'

Suzanne studies the set of his cheek, 'Are you sick, Pesha?'

'Not conventionally so.' Seeing her confusion, he touches her chin. 'Did you know the Pope wouldn't allow Paganini's burial in consecrated ground? They put him in a grave on his own estate. By an orchard. They moved and reburied him over and over. He wasn't ready to go; he had unfinished business.' His voice cracks. 'I'm not ready to go.'

'That's it,' Suzanne stands, takes Pesha's lunch, drops it with what's left of hers into the waste bin behind them. Above the trees, the New York skyline anchors a grey sky. 'I've heard enough about dead Italian violinists. It's time we reminded people you're as great as Paganini ever was, don't you think? Before Max explodes? Come back to work, Pesha.'

Pesha gets to his feet. He kisses her softly. 'There are things beyond my control, my dear. Still, we should preserve Max. I will continue until it becomes impossible.'

The following morning, Max's driver deposits him in front of his building. Behind him, a yellow cab pulls to a stop. A small man wearing a black coat and a black hat with a blue silk band emerges, falls into step beside him. 'Good morning, Max. Please don't fuss,' he says.

Glancing sideways, Max resists the urge to shout. 'Pesha. Thank God. Here's what's happening. We're going to my office. We will sit. We will discuss the Australian tour. Suzanne will give you your itinerary. In two days, you will get on a plane. You will rehearse for three days. Then you will play at the Sydney Opera House.'

They reach the lift. Office workers bunch around them.

'Max, listen —'

'Not here, Pesha.'

The lift doors open.

In Max's office, Pesha sits. Max punches a button on his phone. 'Suzanne, I need you.'

When Suzanne enters, she looks warily at Max, fondly at Pesha.

'Hello, Suzanne.'

'Pesha! Are you all right?'

'These are extraordinary times, my dear.'

Max interrupts. 'Suzanne, I want you to go to Sydney with Pesha. There will be no interviews, no nonsense. We will perform exactly as promised.' He leans towards Pesha. 'There is a fortune invested in this. Are we in control?'

Quietly, Pesha massages the thickened skin on the fingertips of his left hand.

The New York to Sydney flight is long; Suzanne ensures the service in first class is just so. At last, the plane tilts and Pesha presses his forehead to the window. Below, the sun shines on the Harbour Bridge and Opera House. They negotiate customs, avoid waiting media, take the limousine Suzanne has organised to a boutique hotel in The Rocks. The water views are spectacular. Next day, they enjoy brunch in the hotel restaurant then walk around the foreshore to the Opera House. Paparazzi dart around them.

In the concert hall, the Sydney Symphony Orchestra is assembled and chattering. The rehearsal runs smoothly until Pesha breaks off to swing his bow at a shadow. As the conductor pauses and the orchestra fades to silence Pesha gathers himself, says, 'Ladies and gentlemen, I apologise. I was distracted by a draught.'

Each morning, Pesha and Suzanne walk to the Opera House. Every evening, with the lights of the city asserting themselves to their left, and the lights of harbour traffic picturesque to their right, they walk back. Tonight, as they stroll in the gentling dusk after the final rehearsal, Pesha pulls Suzanne to a stop. 'Not yet,' he says, staring ahead.

Suzanne follows his gaze. She sees only commuters rushing for ferries and joggers making their way along the waterfront. Then Pesha begins to cry; alarmed, Suzanne coaxes him forward. At the hotel she guides him past the concierge to his suite. She goes to the dining table, has him sit. She makes tea, sets the brew before him, sits beside him. She waits for him to drink. 'What, Pesha?'

Pesha hesitates, then grasps her forearm. He nods over her shoulder. 'Look ... quietly, now.'

Suzanne looks. 'What am I looking at?'

'*Look.*'

Again, Suzanne looks. Leaning against the far wall is a tall, thin man holding a violin in one hand and a bow in the other. Wide eyed, she gapes at the thin man, at Pesha.

'Quietly,' Pesha encourages her to her feet, holds her firmly. 'Maestro Niccolò Paganini. My friend, Signorina Suzanne Caine.'

'What? What did you say?' says Suzanne.

Pesha cups her face in his hands, pulls her to him, 'We must be brave.' He holds her gaze as she settles. When she nods, he kisses her cheek.

Paganini assesses Suzanne. He places his Guarnerius and bow on the tablecloth, stands at the head of the table.

'It's time, Pesha.' He gestures towards the city lights beyond the balcony. 'Australia is a peculiar choice for the debut, but it will do.'

'Time? For what? What debut?' says Suzanne.

'Hush now, Suzanne. Please,' says Pesha.

'I will not hush!' Suzanne squares her shoulders, jabs a finger at Paganini, 'You will explain what you want.'

'Bravo!' Paganini presses a hand to his heart, turns to Pesha. 'Perhaps your passionate friend might fetch your Guarnerius.' Pesha nods at Suzanne, frowns when she looks set to argue. 'Take the instrument from its case and put it next to mine,' Paganini says when she returns.

Suzanne opens the case, folds back the velvet cover inside. As she places Pesha's violin on the table she is distracted by an indentation on a tuning peg on the maestro's violin; the same indentation appears on Pesha's. She looks more closely. Just above the sound hole, the A string on both violins is frayed in the same place. Suzanne lifts the instruments by their necks, holds them side by side and inspects their backs. Behind the chin rests are identical scratches, fine as hairs. She places the violins on the table, one beside the other.

Paganini presses his fingertips together, flexes his hands. Squinting and concentrating, he brings the instruments together; where there were two, there is now one. Paganini moves it across the table, towards Pesha. 'It is time.'

'I'm not ready,' Pesha says.

Paganini fixes him with black, red-rimmed eyes. 'We have an agreement.'

Pesha shakes his head. When Suzanne touches his arm he pulls away and retreats to the balcony door; beyond the glass, a cruise liner berths in Circular Quay. As Pesha stares out, Paganini moves to the vacated chair beside Suzanne. His gaze caresses her shoulders.

'I'm surprised you haven't told Suzanne how things are, Pesha,' he says.

Suzanne studies Paganini's face; it tapers to a sharp chin. His hollow cheeks and thin lips are framed by dense sideburns and black, shoulder-length hair. She notices the scent of lavender on his clothing, the smell of old things on his breath. 'Why don't *you* tell me how things are?' she says.

Paganini smiles. 'You know, of course, Pesha's father was a rather ordinary musician?' At the window, Pesha makes a choking sound. Paganini glances at his back. 'I rejected him yet he persisted. He said if I couldn't find the skill I wanted in a grown man, I should use his child.' He shrugs.

As Pesha turns from the window, Paganini reaches into his jacket, produces a thick, stained envelope. He extracts the sheets inside and sets them out carefully. Suzanne inspects the pages; each is covered with handwritten music. 'My God, Pesha, do you know what this is?' she says.

Pesha returns to the table, looks over Suzanne's shoulder. 'I know what it is.'

Paganini nods. 'Grigor and I had a bargain. I would split the Guarnerius. Grigor took one for Pesha. Pesha would play for fifty years. When his time was finished he would play this,' he presses his palms to the music, 'on my behalf. Then — to be sure our reputations were never confused, that the attention remained on my work, on me — the Guarnerius would return to me and Pesha would never play in public again. *Finito.*'

Paganini gathers and smoothes his papers. He looks up at Pesha. 'I know what it is to be a master of the violin. I vowed that as long as I lived, my son would never pick one up. I thought it incredible your father would barter you as he did.'

Pesha freezes. 'You go too far.'

Paganini flutters his fingers as though brushing at an insect. Infuriated, Pesha grabs at him. 'Enough!' Paganini says. He disappears, then reappears on the far side of the room.

'You're the devil,' Pesha whispers.

Paganini recoils. He squints, concentrates; Pesha staggers, clings to Suzanne for support. The virtuosi regard one another with disgust.

'It's time for sleep,' Paganini says, eventually.

Suzanne urges Pesha to the bedroom.

'You know, Suzanne,' Pesha gathers himself once again, 'they used to make Paganini-bonbons? Paganini lollies for people to suck on! Now I ask you!'

Paganini's laughter fills the room.

'Take him to bed. Be sure he sleeps. Tomorrow, we work. Tomorrow night, he plays.'

The next morning Paganini tutors Pesha through the intricacies of his twenty-fifth caprice. This, he tells Suzanne, is the finest of his compositions for solo violin — the piece he had raced death to complete. When it became clear he was to be outrun, he had his favourite Guarnerius buried with him.

'They say the twenty-four are the most difficult pieces ever written for violin,' Paganini whispers to Suzanne while Pesha sweats and strives. 'But they are songs for children compared to the twenty-fifth. Finally, I have someone with the genius to perform it.'

'But what happens to Pesha afterwards?' Suzanne asks.

'No matter,' says Paganini.

Suzanne thinks quickly. 'But today, Pesha is what you were. Such a loss!'

'He is nothing like me. No comparison ...' Paganini mutters. 'To hear me play is to crawl to my feet.'

Suzanne looks at Paganini's hawk nose. 'I don't think so.'

All afternoon, Pesha works. For hours, Suzanne taunts and teases. As night falls, Paganini closes the debate.

'Come to me tonight,' he says. 'Provide candlelight.'

When Pesha and Suzanne retire, Pesha falls immediately asleep. Suzanne slips from beneath the sheets into a thick, white bathrobe. She opens the bedroom door, steps into the living room, closes the door behind her. She finds matches, sets a candle into a glass holder. She lights the wick; the darkness shifts. When Paganini appears at the head of the table the flame illuminates his pallor, casts the contours of his face in shadow.

'Turn the chair towards me, please.' He gestures, Suzanne sits. He takes the Guarnerius, moves to the centre of the room, settles the instrument under his chin. He pushes his left hip forward, points his right foot out and away. His eyes roll back; the whites are the colour of old cream. Swaying, he plays on one string only.

The violin resonates like a small, silver bell. The sound captures the light.

Moments pass.

Suzanne finds herself weeping. Aghast, she grasps her chair, fights the urge to crawl to the maestro's feet.

Still, Paganini plays.

Suzanne releases her chair, presses her hands to her chest.

At last, Paganini lowers the violin. Notes settle, disappear. Suzanne wipes her cheeks, stands and reaches for him. Paganini places the Guarnerius on the table, sets the bow beside it. He studies her face, settles himself onto her chair. 'Let me see you,' he says.

In the kitchen, the refrigerator hums.

Suzanne stares at Paganini. When she reaches for the robe's belt and loosens the knot, he tilts his head. Suzanne shrugs the robe from her shoulders. It falls to her feet. The candlelight is soft on her skin. Again, she starts towards him.

'No.' He raises a hand. 'Let me look.'

Suzanne stops; he explores her body, his gaze like breath on her skin. He stands, circles her, pauses, continues. She sighs, closes her eyes. After a time, he steps away, his face etched with despair. 'Thank you. Please cover yourself.'

When Suzanne opens her eyes, Paganini and the Guarnerius are gone. She looks down at her body, caresses her hips and is startled by the new silk feel of her skin. Beads of sweat sit between her breasts. She smoothes the moisture, puts her finger to her lips, tastes lavender. She bends, pulls on the robe and ties it. Curling herself onto the couch, she sleeps.

Before dawn, Paganini returns. He kneels by her head. '*Bellissima*,' he whispers. 'What might have been can still be — in part. Take the instrument. Pesha may play it. But only for you.'

When she wakes early next morning the Guarnerius is on the couch at her feet.

That evening, Pesha carries a music stand onto the Opera House stage. The audience greets him rapturously while a perplexed conductor peers at the stand, wondering at the handwritten sheet music Pesha places there. From the wings, Suzanne witnesses the agitation of the maestro by Pesha's shoulder. The rest of the house sees an interplay of light, bright and dark.

Pesha confers with the conductor who gathers himself, then announces a programme change. Tonight, the Sydney Opera House will host the world premiere of Niccolò Paganini's twenty-fifth caprice solo for violin — to be performed from the original score.

The audience murmurs. Here and there, people worry about apples.

The house lights are cut.

When the first spotlight picks him out, Pesha plays. His shoulders hunch and contort. The Guarnerius sounds like a harp ... a horn ... a woman's scream. Pesha weaves the notes and the silences between them into something unearthly.

Guiding and nudging, Paganini supervises.

It's a six-minute caprice.

When Pesha finishes, the audience weeps, shouts and applauds. Paganini stands with his arms flung wide. The euphoria washes over Pesha like water. He bows, collects Paganini's music, slips it inside the lapel of his tailcoat. He departs the stage. Savouring the moment, Paganini stays where he is. As the lights burn down on him, the conductor waits for Pesha's return. Minutes pass. The audience shuffles. Mortified, the conductor consults with the leader of the orchestra.

In the wings, Suzanne has met Pesha with a change of clothes and suitcases.

The next day, in a hotel suite in Brisbane, Pesha contemplates the Guarnerius as it sits in its case with their luggage. 'They'll come after us, you know,' he says. 'I expect Max is already on a plane.'

Suzanne puts her cheek to Pesha's, slips her arms around him. He takes her shoulders, inspects her face — during the past day she has displayed a startling new sensuality. Suzanne sees his confusion. 'It's all right,' she smiles.

Pesha feels he is watching himself from a great height. 'I love you,' he says, for the first time. Suzanne presses her hand to his cheek. Pesha kisses her palm then bends to unzip the garment sleeve containing his suit from the night before. Reaching into the jacket, he extracts Paganini's score.

'Oh, Pesha,' says Suzanne. 'We can't keep the music.'

'No.' Pesha opens the Guarnerius case, puts the score inside. He picks up the case. 'Or this. Such treasures, such a waste.'

'Not completely,' Suzanne's voice is small. 'I took care of the Guarnerius; it's ours — yours.'

Pesha considers her. 'What did you do, Suzanne?'

'It's fixed, that's all.' She takes his hat from the stand and gives it to him. 'Come on, let's walk.'

In the corridor, Pesha stops as the door to their suite closes behind them. Turning, he swipes their keycard, disappears inside, re-emerges with the Guarnerius and his music stand in its carry bag. Suzanne raises her eyebrows. She takes the music stand from him.

Outside, the streets are named after English monarchs: kings run in one direction, queens in another. Eventually, George Street deposits them at a farmers' market. The city fathers have covered the square with concrete: when the sun shines on it, the place cooks. Still, Pesha and Suzanne discover a pleasing variety of figs and herbed salmon, stop to appreciate music played by Andean men on flute, pan pipe, and mandolin. A stilt walker moves through the crowd like a giraffe.

On a whim, Pesha locates himself under a small tree on the main walkway to the stalls. He takes the Guarnerius from its case, slips Paganini's score into his shirt, opens the case by his feet. Suzanne settles the music stand in its carry bag behind him. Grinning at the joke of it, Pesha plays tangos by Piazzolla, Canaro and D'Arienzo. When shoppers leave the market they're carrying food and loose change. Pesha is like a rock in a rushing stream: people separate around him, give him coins.

Suzanne positions herself by a nearby fruit stand, brings him fresh-made juice in paper cups.

Then Pesha extracts the maestro's score from its envelope and positions it on the music stand. He resettles the Guarnerius under his chin. He blends elements of the twenty-fifth with a Lutosławski partita; immediately, shoppers abandon the stalls to fill his violin case with notes instead of coins. The sun shines hot.

Pesha interprets and invents. The crowd listens and perspires.

Finally, when people are pressed shoulder to shoulder, Pesha presents the twenty-fifth in its entirety. His shoulders hunch and contort. The Guarnerius sounds like a songbird, a weeping child.

As Suzanne bites into a red apple, a pale hand takes it from her.

'*Grazie mille, bellissima.*'

'Niccolò,' Suzanne breathes.

Paganini nibbles neatly, sets the apple on the counter and starts towards Pesha.

'Where are you going?' Suzanne catches his arm.

Paganini stops, winds an arm around her shoulders; he draws her through the crowd. Intrigued by the thin man in the tailcoat and the girl with the cherubic face people press close, anticipating street theatre. Seeing Paganini, Pesha takes the score from its stand and pushes it into his shirt.

'I can't imagine what you think you are doing,' the maestro says when Pesha is close enough to hear. 'To continue when we agreed you would stop is one thing, but to present the twenty-fifth in this, this ...' He gestures at their entranced audience and the surrounding stalls. 'It is too much. You have broken our agreement, Pesha. You must return my gift.'

'Let her go,' Pesha raises his bow. Around them, onlookers tilt their heads.

'The Guarnerius, please,' Paganini reaches for the violin.

Pesha tightens his hold on the instrument's neck; the strings bite into his fingers. 'What gift? What did you do to her?'

'It's not what I did to her. It's what she did for me,' Paganini smiles. The crowd sighs.

'It's not what you think, Pesha,' Suzanne's cheeks shine with tears.

Adrenalin floods Pesha's body. He returns the Guarnerius to its case. Standing, he pulls Suzanne to him, hushes her while Paganini retrieves the violin, turns, and moves away. Quickly, Pesha reaches into his shirt, his eyes fixed on Paganini's back. Grasping the maestro's pages in both hands he pulls and tears, throwing the pieces high. Like dying butterflies they flutter and fall to the ground. People pick up the scraps, study, then souvenir them.

'Niccolò!' Pesha shouts, holding a last scrap between thumb and forefinger. He waves it as Paganini turns. He claps his hands. The paper drops and settles. Paganini stares. Fragments of yellowed paper are scattered on the concrete. He picks up one of the pieces. When he raises his head his face is twisted.

'Are you mad?' he roars.

Around them, the audience applauds. 'Yo!' someone calls. 'Bravo!' someone adds. 'God, the thin man must be hot,' someone else observes. A woman sipping a smoothie through a straw steps forward, drops a coin into the Guarnerius case at Pesha's feet.

'We had an agreement!' Paganini's voice is as thin as a reed. He scans the audience, points at Pesha. 'This man is a cheat. A vandal. A thief! Do you understand what he has taken from you?' He stoops, bellows at a woman with a sun-pinked nose. 'Do you?' She gazes at his lips, leans towards him. 'Or you?' A fat man eating an ice cream looks at his feet. Wildly, he contemplates the crowd's transfixed faces. 'The twenty-fifth caprice! My caprice! Niccolò Paganini's greatest work!' His chest rises and falls; he pants like an animal. 'My God, you people ...' He settles the Guarnerius under his chin. 'This is what he has destroyed ...'

The maestro draws the bow across the strings. At first, there is no sound. His shoulders hunch and contort. He strives and strains. Then, his cheeks fill with colour and sweat appears on his forehead. All at once, the market square is awash with the scent of lavender. The Guarnerius shrieks.

Paganini plays.

The twenty-fifth tears at the audience, pushes into the market stalls and the streets beyond. In the towers surrounding the square, office workers stop, move to windows. The crowd presses closer. Pesha and Suzanne retreat.

'Encore!' someone calls when Paganini finishes. Someone begins a slow, rhythmic clapping. Passers-by stop and wait. Paganini scans the crowd for Pesha and Suzanne: when he sees they are gone, he makes to follow. The audience closes ranks. 'More!' it shouts. The clapping is avaricious and insistent.

Paganini presses his forearm to his head, stares in wonder at the moisture on his sleeve.

He considers the predatory faces surrounding him. Grasping his bow in one hand and the Guarnerius in the other, he succumbs. He repeats the twenty-fifth again and again. The audience demands and encourages. When onlookers leave, they are quickly replaced.

Somewhere between midnight and dawn, the market square cools.

Held fast, the maestro plays.

If even the best-laid schemes o' mice an' men gang aft agley, I'm not sure Sir Edward Jellicoe's scheme ever stood much of a chance ... And he leaves somebody else to clear up the mess: typical bloody aristocrat.

A Whole Bloody Century

Jonathan Pinnock

I don't know why I still do the flowers. It's not as if I believe any more — how could I? — but I suppose someone has to do it. At least it gets me out of the house, and Marianne next door is always happy to look after Amelie for a couple of hours. The vicar's a nice lad, as well. Too young, of course, and completely useless as far as helping us cope with it all. I can't really blame him, though. He's never had kids and between you and me, I doubt if he's even the marrying kind.

But it's a nice little church. We've got some lovely stained glass windows that people come from miles around to see, and you'll often find someone down on their hands and knees making brass rubbings. And there's always a healthy congregation for special occasions, even if it is mostly made up of divorcees showing a bit of leg for the young vicar's benefit. Even though, as I say, they're probably wasting their time.

I didn't hear the door open. In fact, the first thing I was aware of was a chilly draught that raised goose pimples on the back of my neck. I didn't even look up — I had my hands full trying to get some lilies to stand up straight — so I just shouted, 'He's not here!' There was no reply, so I added, 'You can try the vicarage! It's the other side of the car park!'

There was still no reply, although I was certain that whoever had come in was still there, watching me, and it was beginning to feel a little creepy. So I put the lilies down, stood up and turned around. My heart skipped a beat when I saw the tramp standing there, halfway down the aisle. Well, I know it's not terribly politically correct, but it's the only word I can think of to describe him: a tramp. (Or maybe you're supposed to say vagrant these days, are you? It's all so horribly complicated, isn't it?) Anyway, he was absolutely filthy, clothes in tatters and white hair sprouting out all over him. My God, the hair! It was like something you'd see in a zoo. And he was just standing there, a great six and a half foot looming presence, gazing in my direction with his head on one side and a peculiar kind of frown on his face.

We stood there staring at each other for a moment or two as if we were both trying to work out what to do next. 'Can I help you?' I said eventually. He made a sort of grunting sound and then lurched forward, tripping over the edge of one of the pews and falling over. I ran to him, despite myself. He was trying to lever himself up off the floor. 'Are you all right?' I said. He responded by thrashing his head around, as if trying to find the source of the voice. I suddenly realised what was wrong.

'Gosh, you're blind, aren't you?' I said, kicking myself for being so dense.

'Bluurgh ... bligh ... blind,' he muttered back at me, as if he was trying to work out what the word meant. The voice was unexpectedly cultured: a plummy, aristocratic drawl, the voice of someone who'd consumed more than their full quota of fine port and cigars in their time. Not at all the sort of chap you'd expect to see on the High Street trying to push a *Big Issue* in your face. And now that I was closer to him, I could see that although his clothes were indeed ragged and dirty, they would probably have cost a bob or two when they were new; although how long ago that might have been, I hesitated to guess. The style was very old fashioned indeed, but you can't always tell these days, can you? His face was covered in muck, with a long, straggly beard that you could hide most of your lunch in. His disgusting, greasy hair came right down to his chest and he smelt sort of musty, like something that had been kept in the cellar over the winter.

'Blind ... yes, yes ... must be blind,' he continued, with what looked like a fleeting, rueful, smile. He tried to get up once again, and I took hold of his arm to support him. For such a tall man, he was unexpectedly light. Underneath his baggy clothes and facial hair, he must have been as thin as a rake.

'You need a good meal inside you,' I remarked. 'Where do you live? Have you come far? Can I take you there?'

At this, he made a strange 'Gnurggh' sort of noise and threw his head from side to side. I'd obviously said the wrong thing. For a moment, I thought about offering to take him home for some lunch, but I abandoned the idea straight away. It wasn't as if I was particularly afraid of the man any more — he was clearly too weak to hurt a fly — but it wouldn't be fair on Amelie.

'Are you sure you don't want to go home? I can take you in the car,' I ventured.

'N ... no. N ... noooooooooo,' he said, waving his hands frantically in front of him.

'All right ... all right, I'm sorry, I —' He was taking something out of his pocket. It was a small bottle, filled with straw-coloured liquid.

'Elixir,' he said, tapping it with his finger.

'Oh no, we can't have that,' I said. I might have lost my faith, but I wasn't about to condone drinking in Church. I moved quickly towards him, and tried to grab the bottle out of his hand.

'Elixir!' he shouted, snatching the bottle back. 'Elixir!'

'I don't care if it's a hundred-year-old malt, you're not drinking it here!' I said. He seemed to find this very funny for some reason, and he started chuckling bitterly to himself.

'A hundred years,' he said. 'A hundred years.' Then, out of the blue, his voice suddenly rose to a roar. 'A whole bloody century!' he bellowed. 'Can you imagine that? Can you?'

I didn't know what to make of this. The man was clearly deranged. And he still had his hands on the bottle.

'Elixir!' he cried one more time, as I made another lunge for him. This time, I managed to get my hands on it, but I immediately felt the bony grip of his other hand on my wrist. We tussled for several seconds, until finally the bottle flew out of both our hands, turned a somersault in mid-air and then smashed onto the stone floor.

'Well, it's gone now,' I said. But the man was distraught. He put his head back and howled. Then he hung his head and slowly sank to his knees on the ground.

'Gone,' was all he said, shaking his head from side to side. 'Gone.'

I knelt down next to him. 'Look,' I said, 'I'm sorry, but I really couldn't have you doing that here. It's — good Lord, doesn't that hurt?' I'd caught sight of the state of his hands. The fingernails were ground down to nothing, and the fingers themselves were full of splinters. I took the hands gently in mine.

'Mmmmm,' he said, nodding. 'Hurts.' He opened up his palms. The flesh was raw and scarred.

'You need help,' I said, suddenly feeling the need to act. I think something in me clicked at that point. For most of her short time on Earth, my life had been defined as Amelie's 'carer' (and how I hate that word: how could anyone not care?), cleaning her, feeding her, and watching helplessly as her tiny body slowly switched itself off. Here at last was someone I could actually do something for.

'I'll go and get help,' I said, standing up. I patted my pockets to find my phone, and then I remembered that I'd left it in the car. 'Stay there,' I said. 'Don't go away. I'll get help. Okay?'

The man nodded without saying a word and I turned away. I got to the car, and found my mobile. I dialled the number and the voice asked me for fire, police, or ambulance. 'Ambulance,' I said. I explained the situation, and they said that someone would be over soon.

On my way back to the church, I noticed that the cluster of graves up against the right-hand wall looked different from usual. As I walked towards it, I saw that one of the headstones had been knocked over. There had been a spate of young toerags vandalising churchyards recently, and we'd thought ourselves lucky that we'd been left alone.

But when I got there, I found that the damage was worse than I'd feared. One of the graves had actually been dug up, right next to the headstone. There was earth scattered everywhere, along with splinters of wood. One of the splinters had a brass handle attached to it. Why would anyone do this? What kind of sick idiot would do this kind of thing for kicks?

I wondered if the headstone might provide a clue. The dates on it were 1854 to 1913, and the name was Sir Edward Jellicoe, F.R.S. Beneath this, there was the curious inscription 'Beloved Husband of Elizabeth and Seeker of the Divine Secret'. Idly, I turned over one of the pieces of wood. On it were hundreds of tiny scratches. Scratches grouped in fours with a diagonal line through them. I picked up another one. That, too, was covered in regular scratches. With my heart pounding, I realised that every single piece of wood scattered around the grave was covered in markings that could only have been made by a human being.

And then I thought of the tramp's hands. And the more I thought, the more my heart raced. Then I looked at the gravestone again. 1913. A hundred years ago. A whole bloody century. Sir Edward Jellicoe had been under the earth for a whole bloody century.

As a child I'd always been fascinated by the idea of being buried alive. When we were quite small, when I was not much older than Amelie is now, my sister and I found out that we could just about fit in the bottom drawer of my chest of drawers, and we would dare each other to spend as long as possible inside it. At first, it was quite peaceful and calm in there, but after a while the panic started, and I would end up banging on the side for someone to let me out. But what if you were in a wooden box six feet under the earth?

I knew the answer already. You'd scratch and scrape your way to the top, whatever it took. However long it took. Even if it took a whole bloody century.

But that was crazy. No one lives that long, and besides the air would run out in a matter of hours.

Unless there was something keeping them alive.

The Divine Secret.

The elixir of life.

The elixir ...

But it wasn't Sir Edward Jellicoe who came into my mind at that moment. It was Amelie. Maybe I could do something for her after all. Maybe this elixir, whatever it was, could keep her alive? I know it seems preposterous now, but can you blame me for clutching at any speck of winnowed straw dust that wafted past on the breeze?

I raced back to the church, threw open the door and hurled myself towards where I'd left him. But the only thing in the aisle was a pile of moth-eaten old rags that crumbled to dust when I tried to pick them up. The man who had occupied them had vanished, leaving nothing to mark his former presence apart from a dank, earthy scent that lingered on in the air. And as the low winter sun burst through the stained glass windows, it picked out the tiny fragments of his bottle on the stone floor in a glorious rainbow of perfect bright colours. The stain from the liquid had all but evaporated.

Miha Mazzini has a PhD in the Anthropology of Everyday Life from the Institutum Studiorum Humanitatis in Slovenia. Let's hope it didn't involve a viva voce as sad and haunting as the one in this story.

Translated by Lenart Pogačnik

In the Walls

Miha Mazzini

I met her during our company's Christmas party. The managing director's secretary had forgotten to reserve the usual restaurant on time, so they had to rearrange and decorate the passage between our office buildings for a night. No one was particularly upset about this at the board meeting. Our calendars were already filled with holiday parties for partners and customers, present and future ones. During the many years of my career, I had come to recognise the paradox: party after party doesn't make you a party animal. It just makes you numb, tired, and despondent, even depressed.

I drank more than I had intended: not enough to be completely drunk, but too much to drive. Anyway, I wasn't in a hurry. It wasn't one of those Saturdays when the wife comes home from her seminars and the two of us settle the financial sides of our joint life over dinner before retiring to our separate bedrooms.

The younger, and of course lower-ranked, employees crammed themselves into the legal department's office and turned up the music. I kept noticing them as they passed me on their way out for a smoke, some of them returning with slightly wider grins on their faces and smelling of weed, a scent that my generation had learned alongside our schoolbooks. The slightly older staff members, hence middle management, preferred going to the bathroom and returning bright eyed, sometimes even with poorly wiped crescents around their nostrils. Being too old for the former and having an aversion to the latter, I socialised for some time with the other regional directors, and then slowly withdrew past the self-service buffet and stopped before a wall of glass. The city skyline sparkled.

She was standing in the corner, blending into a curtain so that I didn't see her at first.

'Did I scare you?'

I shook my head.

She stepped out from the dark, holding an empty champagne glass between her breasts. Small ones, no bra. Tiny nipple outlines. She was somewhat shorter than me with wide hips and a black dress that tried to look expensive, but certainly came from one of those collections that famous names tailor for department stores. She was average looking, with a hint of darkness at the roots of her bleached hair.

I don't forget faces, I just sometimes have trouble recalling where I first saw them.

She introduced herself and said that she was an assistant secretary; one of the resource management companies (the accepted euphemism for modern-day slave traders) had lent her to us some months ago.

I reassured her that she wasn't bothering me and no, she didn't have to leave. We watched the nightly scenery. The motion of headlights on the asphalt, the pulsing red and green bulbs draped over indoor Christmas trees, rooftops outlined with shining neon strips. We followed an ambulance as it flashed down the road, and when it had disappeared she turned towards me.

'You're one of the few directors I've met that has a life outside of the company — at least, that's the feeling I have about you.'

I couldn't hide my surprise, nor did I want to.

She laughed.

'I've had too much to drink. I'm sorry.'

I motioned that it was all right and turned back to the window. Was that so? I couldn't think of many differences between me and the other directors, although I did turn off my cell phone every night and didn't answer emails at three in the morning, even if I couldn't sleep. And I actually took vacations. I imagined my evening ritual: showering, warming my hot chocolate, reading in bed. Turning off the lights, shifting to the right, then left, and right again into sleep.

'You might be mistaken, although I hope not,' I finally replied. We looked at each other and I asked myself if I wouldn't prefer to call a cab. I used to imagine that with age my lustful desires would relent. I was wrong. I just restrained myself more often now, not because of a weakened libido, but because of the thought: am I capable of listening to yet another life story?

The sex was nothing special, although I didn't have to keep my eyes shut. I sensed something slow inside her, perhaps even tired, and that night I was in a pretty similar state. We didn't talk much and she soon turned off the light. She fell asleep sooner than I did, her hands slipping off my shoulders as I gazed at the two vertical cracks of light coming around the edges of the window shutter. I tried to remember the title of the nearly-finished book waiting for me on my bedside table. Slowly I sank into sleep, only to be woken up by an acid feeling rising from my stomach. I leapt up, thinking that I was about to vomit, but nothing came so I just adjusted my pillow. Once awake, I resumed watching the cracks of light.

A child was coughing in one of the apartments next door. I couldn't pinpoint the sound; it was probably coming from upstairs or maybe from the west side of the apartment building. I felt sorry for him, as I remembered my sons, and especially my little daughter who had been very sensitive and often ill — at least that's what the nanny had often told me, in a strained voice. It had been a long time since they'd left and made their own careers. I met them once a year now, for Christmas dinner, and it always struck me how grown up they seemed.

Sometimes I think I lack that real connection I always imagined parents had with their children, because I was absent so much of their childhood. I missed the time when any kind of closeness could emerge. It's probably true, since I sense that my wife, who was away just as consistently, has the same feeling; even though we never talk about it. But whenever I read the newspapers and count the reports about family-related homicides, I say to myself that it could've been worse. We never went into the depths of each other's hearts, but fortunately we didn't go there with knives either.

The child was coughing so badly that he started to choke. I had a feeling that someone, perhaps his mother, was beside him, calming him with soft words even though I couldn't hear her. I waited for him to cry, but he didn't. I imagined the fever making him stare numbly ahead, and him not daring to relax even in the rare moments when he wasn't coughing.

I don't know how long I'd been awake, but the child did not relent. He accompanied me into my dreams.

She offered me coffee, but I declined. If I had skipped my evening ritual, I definitely didn't want to skip my morning one — and that included tea. The apartment must have been rented to her as a room and a half, maybe even two, even though it was in fact just one large space with a tiny extension, a sort of rectangular appendix into which they crammed the kitchen. I looked through the wrinkled sheets on the double bed, which took up at least half of the place, and made sure I hadn't forgotten anything.

We smiled at each other. Explanations were unnecessary.

'You seem tired, have you slept poorly? Did I snore?'

'No, no,' I said, grinning and quickly kissing her on the cheek. I buttoned up my coat and turned towards the door. 'The child next door was coughing all night, that's all. Poor kid.'

I went down the stairs quickly, and as I glanced back for a moment I was surprised by the look on her face. Had I lingered for a second longer I could've recognised that look, but I didn't want to. I focussed on the stairs resonating beneath my feet.

A little over a week later, I received an unexpected phone call. I lifted the receiver and said, 'Yes? Hello?' a few times into the silence of the line. The display said: 'Secretary 9.' I was suprised that someone was calling me from so low in the hierarchy. Her face appeared before me and I opened my mouth but couldn't remember her name.

'Excuse me ... I wish to see you,' she finally said.

I hung up.

Had I made a mistake? I wouldn't have gotten this far in my career if I didn't possess what is commonly called 'a handle on people.' She was undoubtedly one of those low-energy people who move through their lives at a slow pace, leaving the initiative to others. But she didn't seem like a victim looking for someone to make her unhappy. There were a good number of those, and the worst subgroup was the drama kings and queens who allowed themselves to be led into trouble, just so they could make a scene afterwards and cause tearful suffering. First their own, then that of others.

She wasn't pregnant: during the drive, I'd stopped the cab in front of an open store to buy condoms. She couldn't blackmail me since my wife and I don't concern ourselves with each other's private lives. Career benefits, maybe regular employment with the company?

I drummed my fingers on the desk and moved my palm across it from left to right as if playing a glissando on the piano: a sign that a question intrigued me deeply, yet I lacked enough information for an answer.

After a few days, she brought mail into my office and whispered while placing the letters in front of me.

'I only want a single meeting with you. You don't need to be afraid. I won't tell anyone. It's very, very important, but only to me. Please!'

I looked through my schedule and assigned her my first available opening.

We sat at one of the indoor sections of the bar, a place that I visit whenever I want to extend my day just a little bit more. We both ordered tea. Hers was herbal and mine was green; decaffeinated, since the book I was currently reading wasn't interesting enough to warrant half the night.

She didn't know how to start. She seemed to have lost weight, and the dark circles under her eyes contrasted with her pale skin.

'What's wrong?' I said as gently as possible. I was about to add 'Money?' but reconsidered.

'I would like you to sleep with me again. Just one more time and never again. One more time!'

Her hands were grinding the sugar packets rather than pouring them into the tea. The grains crackled like a snake crawling on sandpaper.

A short 'ha' escaped me, more from surprise than amusement. 'Why?'

It took her a long time to start explaining; she shredded a sugar packet in her hands instead, scattering the crystals about with her fingers.

'You mentioned the child coughing all night long?'

'Yes.'

'The child next door?'

'Probably, I don't know.'

'None of the neighbours have any children; most of them are seniors. In the past week, I visited them all using varying excuses and asked if a child had been visiting them. They said no.'

'And?'

'They also didn't hear the coughing.'

'I'm sorry, I really don't understand.'

Red eyes, flushed cheeks. The whiteness of the skin. Fingers shaking. Maybe she was crazy? I thought about calling my attorney to set up a restraining order.

'I'm sorry, I'm sorry.' Her fingers combed her hair. 'I can't imagine what you must think of me!'

'Put yourself in my position. What would you think?'

She nodded, but too quickly, too eagerly.

'Three years ago my son got sick. He was fourteen months old. They called from the daycare and it was a fever, but not a very serious one so he could wait until I finished up at work. He started coughing in the evening and he kept on coughing during the whole night. His temperature rose, so I called the doctor and he said I should give him medicine to bring his temperature down. It helped, but he kept on coughing. I found some syrup that still had a valid expiration date and it helped him a little, but not really. He struggled the whole night, but towards the morning he calmed down and fell asleep. For the first time, he cried in his sleep, so mildly, so sadly that it broke my heart. I hugged him carefully so I wouldn't wake him, and I kissed him on the cheek. I felt his forehead, and the temperature had dropped. I went back to my side of the bed, thanked God, and went to sleep. I woke up in the middle of the day and he was still asleep. I got up and very quietly made coffee for myself and tea for him. I sat down and waited. I couldn't take my eyes off the shape of his little body under the sheets. Fear crept into me. I never imagined there could be so much of it. *No, it can't be true! He's moving, of course he is. He's breathing.* For a long, long time I couldn't muster the courage. When I jumped up I was next to him with a few steps, but I still tiptoed so as not to wake him. I put my palm on his forehead and he was cold. Ice cold!'

Her body fell forward and she banged her forehead on the table, crying.

A tiny voice within me said it was none of my business, that she was just a one-time adventure and that I could get up and leave. I opened my mouth to express my condolences, even though they would be so insignificant, but then I remembered her face that morning as I'd hurried down the stairs, just after I'd told her about the coughing child.

'What can I —'

She cut me off:

'You were the only one who heard him. The only one. Come, sleep with me and let me hear him too. He was all I had, just him, in my entire life. I felt close to him in a way I never thought possible. Let me hear him one last time, please. Please, one last time to say goodbye to him.'

We looked at each other and a thousand explanations popped up in my head, all logical and plausible. But no one had ever looked at me with such hope in her eyes and put herself so completely at my mercy.

I nodded.

'Tomorrow.'

I cancelled all my meetings and secluded myself in the office. Again and again I tried to recall the moment just after I'd realised what she wanted from me, and before I had conceded. A mixture of feelings and images merged and shifted far too fast for me to put into words. There was the possibility that she had gone crazy from the pain and that I had triggered it with my dreams of the coughing child. But I was certain that I hadn't been dreaming at the time. Where had the voice come from? The more I thought about it, the more I remembered it as strangely omnipresent.

Had a child in fact been visiting that night? Would the neighbours lie? Why?

Had the voice travelled from some other building? How could it have sounded like it was all around us?

Why did I promise her so quickly? There are successful businessmen who boast about the way they analyse and study a situation before making a decision, but I think they're lying. When a ball is flying towards an athlete, he doesn't have time to calculate the angles and parabolas. A businessman also makes decisions in the moment, and then spends the rest of his time finding explanations and justifications.

Even after a whole day of sitting in the office, I still didn't know why I had said yes. Probably I was thinking about my family, how we'd been left untouched by death. We hadn't lived through any great wars, we weren't deprived of anything, no one had died or suffered from severe illness. I looked at the leather armchairs and mahogany desk and filing cabinets in my office, the expensive coat on its hanger; I saw her eyes again, bigger than the overcrowded apartment behind her, and I thought that one night was the least I could offer a stranger.

I stalled my arrival: after work I went to dinner and a movie and then took a walk that was supposed to be long. But I ran into a crowd of shoppers who could barely drag their overstuffed bags around the Christmas trees and poorly dressed Santas giving away fliers for yet more shopping. Soon enough, I gave up and slowly fought my way back to the car. I always keep a small suitcase stashed in the trunk in case I get called away on a business trip.

She was waiting for me, wearing business attire too, and addressed me formally, as if stressing the impersonal nature of our relationship.

She asked if I'd like some coffee, but then dismissed it with a wave of her hand, as if to say that I didn't really want to stay awake for long.

'Do you have tea?' I asked.

After a long time rummaging in the cabinets, she found a box of camomile bags and I accepted a cup, though the taste always reminds me of childhood diseases. Her perfume was too loud and when she moved, it always lingered behind. Her every move conveyed her utter effort and fear that she would do something wrong. Her eyes kept getting bigger and she barely dared to breathe.

'Don't worry, I'll stay,' I tried to comfort her. I thought about holding her hand. I saw my arm lifting, but stopped it immediately, it felt so indecent, and pressed my skin against the cold plywood.

She noticed the motion and whispered:

'If you want sex ...'

'No, no.'

Her shoulders relaxed a little.

There were several pictures of her child hanging on the walls, one right after his birth, with no father in sight. I tried to remember if I had seen any of them after the party; surely not, but it is true that we were a bit more focussed on each other that night. When she went to the bathroom, I took down one of the frames and looked to see if the colour of the paint behind it was any different from the surrounding wall. I couldn't decide, but it didn't matter, since three years was too short a time for such things. She'd probably put the pictures away before going to the party, since she wasn't planning on returning home alone.

I sat on the chair, drinking my tea and avoiding her eyes.

No children's toys anywhere.

Maybe I looked at one of the pictures for too long, the one where the boy was sitting on a sleigh wearing thick, red overalls.

'I said to myself that I had to start over. But after something like that, there is no fresh start,' she said.

I felt the need to say something. I searched for words, but then gave up and simply said:

'I can't imagine what it must have been like.'

I was worried that I had been too blunt, but instead she almost smiled at me.

'I read in the yearly report that you have grown-up children. And a wife. Am I causing you problems?'

I shook my head.

Sometimes our eyes wandered off to the wall clock. Its hands had long since passed the eleventh hour.

Midnight. Was it midnight we were waiting for?

Or were we both uncertain how to perform our individual evening rituals? Mine was tailored for a single person, perhaps a lonely one as well; how could I drink my hot chocolate, go to the bathroom, gargle mouthwash, read a book in bed, shift around three times, and go to sleep in her presence? What did she do on nights when she was alone? Could I really watch her, did I even have the right? To see the banalities which lulled her into a sense of security? We all had them. I looked out the window. Decorations hung over the streets and on a thousand homes. In every one of these homes, people were performing rituals that gave them a sense of timelessness, a sense that they existed, that they lived.

The most terrifying thing about the thought of your own death is the realisation that it is stronger than any ritual.

'I'm sorry,' she said, 'Shall we go to bed?'

I was looking towards the half of the bed where I had lain more than a week ago, when disgust and horror came over me. I imagined layers of bodies on the same spot, her former lovers, and then the child, dying afterwards and making way for more lovers again, including me, my own body. And out of all these people, I was the only one to somehow find a link with the child, his existence and death on that part of the bed somehow coinciding with my visit. Now that I know all this, I thought, how can I re-establish the connection tonight? Will the same mites that fed on all the other bodies once again feast on me? I recalled my father's funeral and then my mother's a few years later. I didn't realise what brought them to mind, until suddenly I knew I was standing over the bed with the same feeling I'd had standing over their caskets: that feeling of regret, knowing the cover was about to close over someone I'd failed to really know. Someone who had failed to know me.

I nodded. Yes, it was bedtime.

We each waited politely for the other to use the bathroom first; she relented and took her pajamas with her. I heard her trying to be as quiet as possible, and upon opening the door she ran to the bed and ducked under the covers, dressed in the plainest and loosest pajamas possible.

I looked at myself in the mirror and wondered what I was doing.

We were lying each on our separate halves of the bed while staring at the vertical cracks of light. My eyes had long since grown accustomed to the darkness and could distinguish the shape of the closet containing her clothes, and the edge of the television beside it.

The sounds of the city: cars in the distance, someone walking down the street and shouting this year's Christmas hit. Ambulances occasionally.

I promised myself that when I heard the newspaper delivery men on their scooters, it would mean morning, and I could leave. I remembered how very much I wanted my own scooter when I was a kid, how I delivered newspapers for a whole year on my bicycle before I saved enough money for an old and badly worn-out model. I smiled at the pride, the feel of the squashed rubber on the handles, the turn of my wrist as I accelerated, the drive, the road disappearing under me ...

My head jerked up.

A child was coughing somewhere.

Had I fallen asleep?

Despite the three-foot distance between us, I felt her body tense. She wasn't sleeping; could she hear him now?

He was coughing, catching his breath, choking.

Goosebumps came over me in a cold wave. An immense tingling danced all over my skin and made me consciously hold my breath and tell myself: 'This is just you. Your fear, your body; nothing they say about ghosts is happening right now. The room is still warm and there's no crawling feeling at the back of your neck.'

The child wheezed and barely caught his breath.

'What is it?' she whispered.

'Can't you hear?'

She carefully lifted her head.

'What?'

'He's coughing.'

'Don't mock me!'

She grabbed me by the shoulder, but then froze in place.

The child was coughing.

She slowly removed her hand, held it above me, and then touched me again.

'My God,' she exhaled, 'you're like an antenna! It's him! Him!'

She shifted onto her side, and so did I.

'Please, let me really hear him, I beg you!'

She clenched my shoulder with all her strength. Her hands tied me up, her legs locked around me, and her body forced itself into mine, merging with me and using a power I wouldn't have thought humanly possible. I've read that atoms cannot really make contact since there is always empty space between them, but that night my bones cracked and I could only breathe if it was in sync with her. Her tears grew cold on my neck. From all sides, the cavities of the building surrounded us, apartments full of lonely people. Just we were one, without even space for thoughts between, just for the child crying inside me.

This story by Joanne Rush, winner of the 2013 Fiction Desk ghost story prize, shows us that history itself is no more or less than the accumulation of ghosts.

Guests

Joanne Rush

They say February is the best month to step on a mine. If it is under enough snow it may not detonate. The snow begins in December, like the first gospel; by February it is several feet deep. It is a matter of record that, on Candlemas night in 1994, a group of women from the village of Lisac, in flight from Mladić's army, crossed the mined snowfields to safety. They did not speak, or they spoke only in whispers. They held the barbed wire apart for each other. Then did they run or crawl or dance, knowing that at any moment the solid ground might buck them into quick oblivion, the snow convert to flames?

It is the first of June, 2011. My husband will be glad the snow is gone, despite the increased risk of being blown up: he found the Bosnian winter very cold. He said so last Christmas, in a rare phone call. He didn't mention Bosnia openly, of course, because the British government has no official presence there. Each time he phones he tells me not to worry. He says he's not in danger, but I know this to be untrue. There are no exact maps of the minefields in Bosnia. Even now, sixteen years after the war ended, a donkey sometimes loses its life; or a child, or a spy.

I met my husband when I was nineteen years old. I had come up to Cambridge from a village in Warwickshire to study Computer Sciences. He had come up from Victoria City, Hong Kong, for the same reason. In Cambridge it is called coming up even if you come down. We were called compscis. Only students of unfashionable subjects were given abbreviations: as well as compscis, there were natscis (Natural Scientists) and asnacs (an acronym for Anglo-Saxon, Norse, and Celtic). When I got to know my husband, he would say these all sounded like animals that hadn't made it onto the ark.

Getting to know him didn't happen at once. There were lots of other compscis, most of them dishearteningly loud, and for a while we hovered shyly on opposite edges of this crowd. We finally met on the last Tuesday of Michaelmas term, in the café of the William Gates building. I often ate lunch there; he rarely did, but the kitchen on his college staircase had been declared unsafe. I found this out because he was behind me in the queue for jacket potatoes. One of the first things I noticed about him was that he breathed in, almost inaudibly, before each sentence: a slight inverted gasp which gave a feeling of urgency to his utterances. I also noticed that his elbows stuck out slightly, and that he had very fine black hair, like a mole.

He asked permission to sit beside me, and conscientiously tucked his elbows in. Then, impelled by the dual forces of hunger and loneliness, he plunged into his potato and his life story. His name was Jon. His mother was English, his father Chinese; he had arrived in Cambridge – which was very beautiful, but the cyclists were suicidal and everyone was on drugs — after a twelve hour flight to Heathrow, eight weeks ago, and he was still living out of a single suitcase; he had sent his other possessions ahead 'by sheep', and they were yet to turn up, though he had called the lost property line 'a tousand times'.

In the weeks to come, I would grow to love the crisp Cantonese consonants that occasionally snuck into his English sentences, and his unsteady phonemes. Already I was entranced by his suitcases, voyaging from Hong Kong to Cambridge by sheep.

What followed our first, word- and potato-filled encounter, was an almost entirely non-verbal companionship. Then as now, Jon preferred computer languages to human ones, and most of the time I found this restful, but it did make things harder when we were apart. He particularly disliked telephones. So what stands out most brightly in my memory of the summer at the end of our first year, when I returned unwillingly to my parents in Warwickshire, and he went home to Hong Kong, is the day he sent me a postcard of Victoria Harbour with two lists on the back:

Things we like
1. *Quiet*
2. *King's College Chapel*
3. *Different sides of the bed*

Things we dislike
1. *Bicycles on pavements*
2. *Weed*
3. *Crowds*

Beside the second list was a pencil sketch of an ark, in which were two blobs. In case I should mistake these for his still lost suitcases, or even the miscreant sheep, he had printed below them: COMPSCIS.

'What do you feel about mmharriage?' Jon asked me, at the beginning of our fourth year in Cambridge. (He doesn't stutter, but with certain English words he sometimes fumbles a catch.)

We planned a very modest ceremony. His parents couldn't come – they didn't like flying – but mine were there: my father gruff, my mother querulous. She had already made plain her feelings about my mmharriage to 'a half yellow man'.

'Of course I'm not racist, dear,' she said, a number of times. 'It just that he's so quiet. Don't you want someone more like us?'

1. Quiet, I thought. *2. King's College Chapel. 3. Different sides of the bed.*

Things did get more complicated later on, but I never doubted the soundness of this basis for love.

Jon's supervisor took him aside a few weeks before we graduated. She had been asked to recommend someone for a job at GCHQ. 'Legalised hacking,' she called it: exactly the sort of thing he'd be good at. I was already planning to set up as a freelance web designer, and neither of us wanted to face London. So we moved to Cheltenham Spa.

Our shabby third-storey flat was not a castle, unless of the air. It had white stuccoed ceilings, quietly peeling, and few comforts at first beyond a second-hand dinner table and a very low futon bed. Nevertheless we were happy there.

For two years Jon was deskbound in Cheltenham. But twelve months ago he was invited to a meeting about an important operation, co-run with the Americans, which needed someone in precisely his field of expertise. If he agreed, he'd be stationed at an old British military base in Bosnia. They couldn't say exactly how long for. My husband is a man of principle: he does things he doesn't want to do because he feels he should. I've got fewer principles: I just hoped it wouldn't take long.

Jon left for Bosnia in June 2010. That summer I kept myself busy, working from home. My job meant I spent a lot of time on the phone, explaining to clients the difference between mythology and technology, turning their dreams and visions into navigable sites — I'm not an imaginative person, but I'm good at detail. I got through one day at a time.

At the end of our street was a coffee shop, which was Polish and sold astonishing cakes. When the flat felt too empty I worked there instead. The waitress wore a black panelled apron with DONT ASK written across it in wobbly white velcro letters, or sometimes ASK ME L8R. 'Wait one minute,' she'd say. '*Sernik* arrives from kitchen.' This was often the closest I got to a real conversation all day.

When I wasn't working, I went for long walks. Sometimes I walked past GCHQ, that vast blister of glass and concrete on the edge of the A40. I'd been told it had a street inside, and a computer room the size of the Royal Albert Hall. Jon's face appeared in there each day, pixelated, on a plasma screen. 'Good morning Cheltenham,' he'd say. 'See and hear you fine.' Then he'd vanish, replaced by a man in Beirut or Kabul.

Autumn came, then winter. The waitress in the Polish café said I was looking peaky, a word she'd recently learnt. I stopped going there so often: I didn't like people fretting. But I still took long walks, sometimes right up into the Cotswolds. On these walks I allowed myself to picture Jon. I did this cautiously, small bits at a time. His hands. The blurred edge of his jaw. Never whole.

I spent Christmas alone, after some deliberation. In the morning I ate half a croissant and started crying. The tears took a long time to stop. At four o'clock Jon phoned. 'Happy Christmas,' he said. He sounded far away. He asked me how I was, and I told him I was fine. 'It's very cold here,' he said. We talked for a stilted quarter of an hour. He said, 'Take care of yourself. I love you.' Then he added quickly, 'Listen, I may be onto something. I can't explain on the phone, but it might mean I'm back soon.'

'I hope so,' I said. I put the receiver down, expecting to feel happy. But instead I felt more sad. My husband didn't know that leaving someone could not be put right simply by coming back to them. Delicacy, filaments, were beyond him. He had strong hands, but that meant his forte was lifting heavy objects: small things slipped through his fingers, fragile things cracked in his grip.

When Christmas was over, I had a stroke of luck. A maritime museum in the south of England commissioned me to design a website. Charles, the man I spoke to on the phone, said they didn't want to use templates: everything must be bespoke. It was a challenging project; it would take three or four months to complete. I was anxious to begin.

A few days after that I ran out of milk, and popped into town for more. When I got back, there was a diminutive old lady in a headscarf standing in my kitchen, grinding coffee in a brass mill. At her elbow was a small copper jug. '*Dobro jutro*,' she said. Her smile was animated, but she was clearly dead.

Over the weeks that followed, unaccommodated ghosts filled the flat. The oldest arrived first, shapeless, clutching suitcases. They came from Mostar, Sarajevo, Banjaluka, from eighteen years ago. They had walked past engines blown out of vehicles and the half-cremated remains of other human beings, they had fallen over cliffs, stepped on mines, and been shot with guns — in the eye neatly once or the back many times. They had borne most, without a doubt, so it was not up to me to question where they chose to put it down.

It was a busy time for me. Charles phoned several times a week to discuss my progress, which was never fast enough for his taste. But it was nice to have company when I finished work in the evenings, and mostly the ghosts were no bother, though sometimes they moved things and it took me a while to find them. When I walked past they reached out to touch me. Their hands grazed my shoulder, tugged on my hair. None of this was malicious: all they wanted was my attention.

At first their conversations were unintelligible to me, like the lyrics of music that is playing in another room. But over time the words separated out and acquired meaning.

When they perceived this, the *gosti* — ghosts, guests — became more demanding. They needed paprika, they needed clean towels. They needed someone to listen to them, and who else was there?

In spring more ghosts arrived: mostly men. They appeared to be waiting for something, and to ease this process they got hold of my husband's single malt whisky. They also smoked constantly, dropping the butts on the carpet. I don't mean to be rude, but it wouldn't have killed them to use an ashtray.

As the flat filled up, it was the living room that attracted the greatest number of ghosts. The fumes from home-grown Bosnian tobacco mixed with the earthy smell of American cigarettes accepted as bribes or bought on the black market: Smokin' Joes and Camel Reds were passed across my coffee table by card-playing Muslim soldiers whose fingers were stained pollen-yellow with nicotine. '*Čmaru jedan*,' they muttered. '*Baja pojela ti jaja.*' You arsehole. I hope a bug eats your balls. When they were winning, they switched to old battle songs. 'The scent of lilies fills the meadow,' they hummed under their breath. On the other side of the room a dead Serb glared.

One of the ghosts, a young boy, stood apart by the TV. My attention was drawn to him because of his wing-like elbows, which reminded me of Jon. He was clutching a bass guitar, although his hands had been destroyed by a shell.

'That one is my grandson.'

It was the old woman with the coffee pot, the one from the first day; she'd walked through the wall beside me. I wished they wouldn't do that: it left marks.

'He's a good boy, but I don't like his music — all that banging and shouting. You want a little coffee? Yes you have time. Sit here next to me.

'Tchk! Look at this. My doctor calls them liver spots. I said to him Doctor, it looks to me like I'm going mouldy. He gives me cream for them but I don't like to use it, Allah never meant for us to cure old age.

'Now Tarik, that grandson of mine, he's a Muslim but you wouldn't know it. I've seen him drinking šlivovica, he even eats sausage rolls. Well like his daddy he was raised in Sarajevo so it's not surprising. Young people there just glue their eyes to the West, it's always been that way. Tarik's in a rock band with three older boys I don't like much. They call themselves *Histerija*, and worship some London noiseniks by name of Led Zep Lin. The only time I went to one of their concerts I had to put my hands over my ears. "*Ja sam budućnost*," they kept on shouting. Such nonsense. I think all the jiggling about was meant to be dancing, but it looked more like some kind of fit.

'Just a few weeks after that the siege started. You know, every morning of my life I'd woken up to the tram bells, but on that day they stopped dead and didn't ring again for three years. It seemed like everything stopped, even gravity. Snipers were killing people in the streets, and by the time anyone dared go out for the bodies they'd got stiff. I'll never forget how the arms stuck out and the heads twisted sideways instead of flopping. Or the shelling either: it was like that rock concert all over again.

'My husband, may Allah rest him, left the house each evening to stand on the street with other Sarajevan men and talk. Those poor men looked worse than the dead and no wonder: they'd eaten bread made of oats, then of the stalks of hazel bushes, then of ground apple skins. They said the West had forgotten us, but it's my opinion the West never knew we existed. Of course Tarik listened to them. He knew he was a Muslim by then, surely enough: he thought he'd grow up into arms. But I sent him out to buy beans the day the mortar hit Markale market in February '94, and sixty-eight people died. That shell blew off both his poor hands, though what killed him was the fragment that got buried in his skull.'

Tarik stood in the corner of my living room, clutching his guitar. 'I am the future,' he whispered. Angry chords curled around him. '*Ja sam buducnost.*'

'Motherfucking Chetnik!'
'Sisterfucking Turk!'
The coffee table across the room from us collapsed, and playing cards swooped through the air like startled birds. Two red-faced men in black leather jackets squared up to each other: the glaring Serb had tripped over a card player's foot. I thought they were going to fight, but the card player's friends grabbed him by the shoulders and the Serb allowed himself to be shunted back to our side of the room, grumbling loudly and cracking his knuckle-tattoos into his palms.

Such eruptions were frequent, especially at first. 'You did this,' the ghosts accused each other. 'You did that.' But their voices were tired: it was hard for them to remember which flag to kiss and which to burn. The elderly ghosts were happier recalling their vegetable gardens than their disputes; they sat together to drink šlivovica and reminisce. And the soldiers from different armies exchanged cigarettes more often than blows. So in my living room Bosnian Muslims, Catholics, Orthodox Christians, and Sephardic Jews gathered and pooled like drops of water.

In March or April — I'm not sure which — Charles began to call more persistently, wanting to know when the website would be finished. 'Is something wrong?' he said. Eventually I took the phone off the hook.

I barely left the flat, even to buy food. Instead I ate what the ghosts cooked. They filled my kitchen with the smell of lamb frying in garlic and paprika; then they got distracted, by an argument about politics or ingredients, and burnt the bottoms of my pans. I did sometimes go out, to get things they had forgotten: tomatoes, an egg. But those times were getting rarer. The light was too bright, the people too solid; their voices reached me from a long way away, like sounds heard underwater. I preferred to devote myself to the ghosts: their recipes and whims, their stories.

So I was there when Lejla walked in. Though barely more than a child, she was visibly pregnant. She leant against the living room wall, just inside the threshold, holding her heavy belly in her hands.

'Pass that cushion dear? *Ouf*, that's better. At my age a body has too many bones and they all get closer to the surface.'

It was Tarik's grandmother again, clutching her eternal coffee pot. 'That poor child,' she said. 'She's a Croat, see the dinky gold cross? It's a wonder she held onto it. I've just this minute been chatting to a woman who was locked up with her in Banjaluka. She's making chicken liver pilaf if you want some later.'

This was Lejla's story, as told to me by Tarik's grandmother, who heard it from the ghost in my kitchen, who saw it with her own eyes.

She was a nice girl from a good Croat family, who didn't decide to get out of the newly declared Republic of Serbia quickly enough. So she was separated from them and held in a makeshift prison camp next to the police station.

At night there were rapes. Guards with flashlights, or just torches made of lighted paper, searched for anyone who was young and female.

They used a knife to cut her dress open. Then they raped her many times in one night. She was thirteen years old. When she became pregnant they continued to rape her nightly.

Eventually they put her in a train wagon meant for cattle but crowded with Croat women and girls. The train travelled south to the foot of Vlasic mountain. When it ran out of track, buses took them the rest of the way up. Lejla joined an interminable line of people: heads down, shuffling, sometimes stumbling, but moving slowly towards free Bosnia, or so they hoped. The road cut into the side of the mountain was narrow, and there were corpses on the rocks below. At some point in the night she tripped and joined them.

In my living room, she — Lejla — listened shyly to the music that came from Tarik, the handless guitar-playing boy. She moved towards him so slowly she did not seem to be moving at all. But she was.

'Jimmy Page,' she said quietly.

He frowned. 'John Paul Jones.' He had a memorable voice for a boy: gravelly, smoke-scarred.

'Is he better?'

'I prefer bass guitar.'

'I do too.'

It wasn't long before the Muslim boy with the shell-broken hands was deep in conversation with the raped Croat girl.

She did tell him some of what had happened to her. Shutting her eyes, touching the raised bumps of the wallpaper with one hand. But mostly they talked about rock music. He was enthusiastic about the electric guitar of Plavi Orkestar; she giggled. 'They dance like chickens,' she said. 'They hug turkeys in their videos.' She mentioned the plangent music of Crvena Jabuka; he thought it was wet. 'You may discord,' he said politely. But she did not discord with him, not at all.

I watched her a lot, I admit. She was so young. I worried about how she would cope with motherhood: how could a child look after a child? Sometimes I forgot that they were both already dead.

I stopped work on the maritime museum's website. When I was not watching Lejla and Tarik, I went into the kitchen and helped the older ghosts cook: I peeled their potatoes, I rubbed flour and lard together to make pastry. Or I sat at the breakfast bar and listened to them talk. All the ghosts were keenly interested in the search for General Mladić, the Bosnian-born Serb who had led an army through their country; most of them were angry at how long it was taking.

'He's in Serbia.'

'He's not in Serbia at all, he's in Montenegro.'

'He's escaped Europe altogether by now.'

'That butchering peasant.'

'What occupies him these days?'

'He used to keep bees.'

'No doubt he still jeers at his goats.'

'The ones he named Major and Mitterand and Kohl?'

'Yes, after those Western politicians he so despised.'

'His health too must be much on his mind.'

'He's old by now.'

'So would I be, but for him.'

'So would we all be.'

At first the ghosts were easily distracted from the manhunt. They compared the size of their gardens, or the size of the peppers they had grown in their gardens. They had aimed to sit on a porch swing through summer evenings, but into their modest ambitions had blundered Mladić. He had shelled their houses and mined their vegetable patches. He had said: 'I shall be vindicated by history.' They were his dead.

Then, last Thursday, I came downstairs to find all the ghosts clustered round the television, jostling each other for the best view. As I watched, the screen fizzed and spat, and my husband appeared. It was definitely him: his pointy elbows, moley hair. The ghosts nudged me slyly, but then the picture flickered and Jon was replaced by a man with a polka-dot tie and greased-back hair. 'Kruno Standeker, the journalist,' Tarik's grandmother whispered to me. 'He was killed by a road mine near Mostar seventeen years ago.'

'Ratko Mladić,' intoned Standeker, 'was born in Bosnia in 1942. He went to military school in Serbia and entered the Yugoslav army, rising to the rank of Colonel General. When Bosnia declared independence in 1992, he blockaded the city of Sarajevo and shelled it for four years. In 1994, he allegedly ordered the genocide of over eight thousand Muslims in Srebrenica.'

The screen filled with soundless black-and-white footage. The war was over, and Mladić — ears sticking out beneath his peaked cap — was retreating to Serbia, where he lived in army barracks, going openly to football matches and horse races. Then the political atmosphere turned against him and he was on the run in Han Pijesak and New Belgrade, moving every two or three weeks between housing estates whose walls were covered with spray-paint vampires and signatures like coils of barbed wire. Serbia put a price on his head; international arrest warrants were drawn up. He left the overpopulated cities and went to live in the country, in a village of plum tree orchards and pepper fields, in a farmhouse made from clay bricks. He had mistaken boredom for safety; he thought no one would look for him there. Even so, he went out only at night. It was as if he had become one of the graffiti vampires from the housing estate walls, as if light petrified him.

For as long as he could remember, Mladić had been a skilful chess player, winning games across the length and breadth of Bosnia: in prison camps, at military headquarters, on the front lines. Now he sat before the chessboard, hour after hour, while an invisible foreigner — a man with electronic eyes and ears — chased his pieces across the black and white squares.

Mladić lived, fortified by obscurity, with cousin Branko, his Glorious Defender: his castle, of course. But most of his pawns — the army, the police, the secret services — had already been taken, the treacherous bastards, they'd gone over to the other side. And now his queen was under threat, his wife Bosiljka suddenly detained and questioned; harassed, beset, while he, helpless, fumed. Even his son — his slick-wheeled, Dacia-driving knight — was closely watched: it was too dangerous to see him much.

The screen spurted into Technicolor, revealing a woman sitting upright at a virtual desk. 'DAWN RAID,' she reported, and the ghosts inhaled a collective gasp. They'd been channel-surfing since the news broke — they knew the story off by heart, in all its permutations — but this was their favourite part. 'MEN IN MASKS MOVE IN,' they mouthed in perfect synchronicity with the woman on the screen, working their mandibles hard. Ten plain-clothed policemen or twenty special officers, armed or unarmed, depending which broadcaster you picked. Mladić was on his way to the garden for a pre-dawn stroll, or he was sitting in his front room wearing a tracksuit. He was handcuffed or he was not handcuffed; he was made to sit in the yard or he was taken into the house. He definitely offered his captors some home-made plum brandy. 'Checkmate,' he conceded politely. 'Which one of you is the foreigner?'

I started to understand.

'High-tech surveillance and tracking techniques were behind this operation,' the reporter was saying primly. 'The British and American intelligence services have been formally thanked for their assistance. Also Bakir Izetbegović, the Muslim member of Bosnia's tripartite presidency, has announced that the arrest was completed with the support of Bosnian security agencies.'

Was that what my husband had been doing? Hunting down the butcher of Srebrenica, bringing the man who called himself God to justice for crimes against humanity? Of course — it must be. Why else would the ghosts have come here?

All day long my guests were jubilant: they twittered and squeaked. They wanted a banquet, a celebration: they wanted, when it came down to it, a wake. Most of them also wanted to keep watching television, so although I'd have liked to see if Jon reappeared, I offered to help in the kitchen.

The first thing we made was *bosanski lonac*, as this would take five hours to cook. We layered chunks of lamb and potato with vegetables including cabbage and peppers, added garlic cloves and chopped parsley, seasoned it generously, and poured white wine and stock over the top. I turned on the gas and brought the oven up to temperature, then placed the stew carefully on the bottom shelf.

The ghosts showed me how to make *sarmas* while the stew was cooking, rolling grape leaves around tiny portions of rice and meat. Once or twice someone opened the oven, and the kitchen filled with the warm, heavy smell of lamb and the floury sourness of half-cooked potatoes. Whenever that happened, cigarette-smoking soldiers appeared in the kitchen to ask how long it would be. The cooks shooed them out. They made *baklava* ahead of time: spreading honey onto filo pastry and adding rosewater to crushed pistachio nuts. The air filled with a back-of-the-throat sweetness and another smell I couldn't identify, which made me uneasy.

I went into the living room to get away from this smell, and also to check what was happening on the news. It's a good thing I did, because soon after that there was an almighty crack as the oven exploded in the kitchen. I remember being lifted off the ground by the force of the explosion, and the sound of glass smashing; then nothing until the siren-scream and epileptic blue lights of the ambulance.

So that's it. I am in bed in a private room in Gloucestershire Royal Hospital. I have concussion and two broken ribs, and the doctors put me on a drip when I first came in because I was badly emaciated. They said that firemen had been over the wreckage of my kitchen and found nothing but a few pieces of an empty pot in the oven; they suggested I had barely eaten for weeks or months. I know they wanted me to concede that I let the gas build up to dangerous levels on purpose, triggering the explosion in a cry for help. But I survived because I was in the living room not the kitchen, and gas doesn't explode by itself. It must have been a spark from one of the soldiers' cigarettes: they kept looking in the oven to see if the stew was done.

When I pointed this out to the doctors, they said it might help if I wrote down what I remembered of the last few months. I've been happy while doing this. The ghosts were always telling me their stories, so I think it is what they would have wanted, too.

And now I'm told my husband will be coming back from Bosnia soon. One thing is certain: Jon won't see the funny side of me being the one to get blown up. When he goes away he says *be safe*, by which he means *safer than normal*, because if something happens to me he won't be here.

About the Contributors

Jason Atkinson is an American writer and musician, now living back in the US after three years in Italy. His stories also appeared in *Various Authors* and *All These Little Worlds*, the first two Fiction Desk anthologies.

Linda Brucesmith is the principal of Aqua Public Relations based in Brisbane, Australia. She has worked as a journalist in Sydney, Melbourne, and on Queensland's Gold Coast. Her short fiction has been published in Askance Publishing's 2013 *Homes Anthology* (Cambridge), and *Andromeda Spaceways Inflight Magazine* (Australia). She won the Fellowship of Australian Writers' Mornington Peninsula Prize 2013, was shortlisted for the Katharine Susannah Prichard Foundation's 2013 KSP Speculative

Fiction Awards, highly commended in the 2012 Fellowship of Australian Writers National Literary Awards and long-listed in the 2012/13 Fish Short Story Prize.

Oli Hadfield is currently studying the MA Writing course at Sheffield Hallam University, where he is a short story editor for *Ink. Magazine* and the deputy editor-in-chief for *Matter*. Outside of his job as a bartender in Sheffield City Centre, he spends his spare time writing short stories, poetry, and film reviews.

Matthew Licht is the author of the detective trilogy *World without Cops*, and several other novels. His short story collection *The Moose Show* (Salt) was nominated for the Frank O'Connor Prize. A new collection, *Justine, Joe & The Zen Garbageman*, is due out soon, again from Salt. He's obsessed with bicycles. Due to this, or as a consequence, he lives in Italy. "Got to burn off the spaghetti somehow."

Matthew's story 'Dave Tough's Luck' appeared in *Various Authors*, the first Fiction Desk anthology. 'Across the Kinderhook' appeared in *Crying Just Like Anybody*.

Amanda Mason is a graduate of Dartington College of Arts, where she studied theatre and began writing by devising and directing her own plays. After a few years of earning a very irregular living in lots of odd jobs, including performing in a comedy street magic act, she became a teacher and has worked in the UK, Italy, Spain, and Germany.

She now lives in York and writes plays, flash fiction, and short stories, often choosing subjects that are dark, strange, and somewhat scary. She is currently working on her first novel.

Miha Mazzini is a Slovenian author, with 27 published books, translated into nine languages. His work has often been anthologised, including in the 2011 Pushcart prize anthology. He's also a screenwriter and director, and voting member of the European Film Academy. He has a PhD in Anthropology of Everyday Life.

Julia Patt is an ex-legend tripper and perennial grad student living in the US. She holds an MFA from the University of North Carolina at Greensboro, where she was a fiction editor for *The Greensboro Review*. She currently edits *7x20: a journal of twitter literature*. Her young adult novels — *i was a fourth grade zombie slayer* and *Through Waterless Places* — were both shortlisted for Mslexia's 2012 Children's Novel Competition, and her short fiction has appeared or is forthcoming in such publications as *Phantom Drift*, *The Fabulist*, and *Modern Grimmoire*.

She lives in Maryland, where she attends the Graduate Institute at St. John's College and updates cemetery records for her local Historical Society.

Jonathan Pinnock has written all sorts of stuff and has been published all over the place, including the BBC. His novel *Mrs Darcy versus the Aliens* (Proxima, 2011) was followed by his Scott Prize-winning short story collection *Dot Dash* (Salt, 2012). He is currently trying to work out what to write next.

Joanne Rush is currently working on a novel about Bosnia, and has just returned from a research trip to the Balkans. She has a PhD from Cambridge University in Renaissance literature. She now lives in London, where she divides her time between teaching and writing.

Eloise Shepherd is a fiction and games writer with a surprisingly successful sideline in competitive boxing. You can read more of her work in Picador's *New Writing 13*, Stories from *Another London Volume 3* and on the Ether Books app. She lives in Peckham and is regularly accesible via social media at @faithlehanne and on her blog www.isthisgaming. wordpress.com. Her mum would also like her to note that she's a Cambridge English graduate, and regularly eats five portions of fruit and veg a day, which balances out all the less parentally appealing gaming, boxing, and tattoos.

Richard Smyth is an author and journalist. His stories have appeared in *.cent*, *The Stinging Fly*, and *Vintage Script* and are read regularly at the Liars' League in London. He has published two non-fiction books: *Bum Fodder*, an illustrated history of toilet paper, was released by Souvenir Press in November 2012, and *Bloody British History: Leeds* was published by the History Press in 2013.

As a journalist, he has written features for *New Humanist*, *History Today*, and *New Scientist magazines*, among others.

He is represented as a novelist by Peter Buckman at the Ampersand Agency.

Ann Wahlman spent her formative years in New England. She holds a degree in Psychology from The Catholic University of America in Washington DC, and received her Master's in Writing from Johns Hopkins University in 2012. Ann lives with her husband in the Maryland/Washington Metropolitan area. Her work has appeared in *Bluestem Magazine*, *Wilderness House Literary Review*, and most recently in *Gargoyle Magazine*.

For more information on the contributors
to this volume, please visit our website:

www.thefictiondesk.com/authors

Also from The Fiction Desk:

The Maginot Line

the third Fiction Desk anthology

New stories by:

Benjamin Johncock	Matt Plass
Ian Sales	Shari Aarlton
Claire Blechman	Mandy Taggart
Andrew Jury	Justin D. Anderson
Harvey Marcus	

ISBN 9780956784346

Crying Just Like Anybody

the fourth Fiction Desk anthology

New stories by:

Colin Corrigan	Mike Scott Thomson
S R Mastrantone	Miha Mazzini
Die Booth	William Thirsk-Gaskill
Matthew Licht	Luiza Sauma
Matt Plass	Richard Smyth

ISBN 9780956784360

Avilable to order from all good British bookshops,
or online at www.thefictiondesk.com.